Volume I

by Debbie Dadey
and
Marcia Thornton Jones

illustrated by John Steven Gurney

SCHOLASTIC INC.

New York Toronto London Auckland Sydney
Mexico City New Delhi Hong Kong Buenos Aires

Vampires Don't Wear Polka Dots, ISBN 0-590-43411-X,
copyright © 1990 by Marcia Thornton Jones and Debra S. Dadey.

Werewolves Don't Go To Summer Camp, ISBN 0-590-44061-6,
text copyright © 1991 by Marcia Thornton Jones and Debra S. Dadey.
Illustrations copyright © 1991 by Scholastic Inc.

Leprechauns Don't Play Basketball, ISBN 0-590-44822-6,
copyright © 1992 by Debra S. Dadey and Marcia Thornton Jones.

Ghosts Don't Eat Potato Chips, ISBN 0-590-45854-X,
copyright © 1992 by Debra S. Dadey and Marcia Thornton Jones.
Illustrations copyright © 1992 by Scholastic Inc.

12 11 10 9 8 7 6 5 4 3 2 1   4 5 6 7 8 9/0

Printed in the U.S.A.   40

This edition created exclusively for Barnes & Noble, Inc.
2004 Barnes & Noble Books

ISBN 0-7607-5878-6

First compilation printing, August 2004

Vampires Don't Wear Polka Dots

To Steve and Eric for your support, and to children everywhere for your inspiration.

M.T.J. and D.D.

1

A New Teacher

"Poor Mrs. Deedee," said Melody. "I feel sorry for her." A couple of other girls in the third-grade classroom at Bailey Elementary School agreed.

"She got what she deserved." Eddie, the class bully, was a tall kid with curly red hair.

Melody turned to Eddie. "You shouldn't have been so mean to her. If you had been nicer she wouldn't have gone crazy!"

"It's not my fault," Eddie said. "Nobody else was very nice to her either."

It was true. There was not an innocent person in the whole class. Every student there had talked out loud or thrown paper wads or done something to drive their teacher crazy. Mrs. Deedee had not actually gone nuts, but she had quit her job after she found her top desk drawer full of shaving cream.

She had been looking for a pencil when she stuck her hands in the mint-scented shaving cream. "I can't stand it any-more!" Mrs. Deedee screamed. She held her hands up like a surgeon and looked around the room. A wild look came into her eyes.

"I don't know who did this, but I want

you to know that you will pay for it. Someday, you'll get yours! Somebody, somewhere, will make you pay!" She laughed a cackling kind of laugh and left the room.

No one in the third grade had seen Mrs. Deedee since, but it was rumored that she had moved to a small town in the farthest corner of Alaska.

Today, the third grade of Bailey Elementary was getting their new teacher. No one had seen her yet and everyone was worried.

"What if we get a male wrestler?" Melody twisted one of her jet black pigtails. "My cousin's teacher moved away, and they got this male wrestler for their new teacher."

"Oh, be serious, Melody," Howie laughed and wrinkled his freckle-covered nose. "Wrestlers don't become teachers!"

"I *am* serious. He weighed at least 300 pounds and had muscles the size of watermelons. He threatened to stuff anybody who misbehaved inside their pencil boxes."

"Did he ever do it?" Howie asked.

"No. He never had to. Nobody ever misbehaved," Melody answered. Everybody agreed that having a male wrestler for a teacher would be a lot worse than having Mrs. Deedee.

A short girl named Liza spoke up. "Maybe we'll get Miss Viola Swamp." Everybody laughed. Viola Swamp was a character in a book they had read.

Liza turned bright red. "Well, we might get her for a teacher and then you'd all be sorry!" That silenced everyone. Viola Swamp was the strictest, meanest teacher in the whole world. If they got somebody like her, they would all be doomed.

"Don't worry," Eddie bragged. "I can

take care of any teacher — even a male wrestler!"

Footsteps from out in the hall made everybody scramble for their seats. An uneasy quiet settled over the class as the footsteps stopped in front of the third-grade room. A couple of students took deep breaths as the doorknob slowly turned.

2

Mrs. Jeepers

Their principal, Mr. Davis, walked into the classroom with a beautiful lady. "Good morning, students," the principal said. Mr. Davis looked something like an egg with two legs. He wore dark-rimmed glasses and was completely bald. "I would like to introduce you to your new teacher, Mrs. Jeepers."

Mrs. Jeepers smiled at the class and said in a strange accent, "It is very nice to meet you, boys and girls. I am sure we are going to have a good year together."

Some of the girls in the back of the room giggled at her accent and Mr. Davis looked at them sternly. "I am sure that no one in the class will give you trouble, Mrs. Jeepers. If they do, I want you to let me know."

"Thank you, Mr. Davis. I am sure we will be fine." Mrs. Jeepers smiled an odd little half smile.

The door closed with a loud click as Mr. Davis left. All twenty-two children looked at Mrs. Jeepers. She was kind of short and her long red hair was pulled back with a purple barrette. She wore a starched white blouse with a high collar. At the collar was a green brooch the size of a chicken egg. It seemed to glow whenever she moved. Her skirt was black and hung to the tops of her black, laced, pointy-toed boots.

While the class stared at her, Mrs. Jeepers looked around the room. A couple of kids were chewing gum and almost everybody slouched in their chairs. A fat boy picked his nose and a girl in the back combed her long blonde hair. Loose papers and books were scattered all over the floor.

Mrs. Jeepers cleared her throat and spoke. "I am glad to be your teacher and I think we should start off by laying the groundwork. There are some rules I expect you to follow."

A few kids in the class groaned.

"Do not worry. They are not difficult rules. They are probably ones that you have already been following. We will start with the most important ones." With that, Mrs. Jeepers proceeded to write three rules on the board.

1. Act nicely to teachers and fellow students.
2. Talk at appropriate times.
3. Walk.

Eddie waved his hand in the air. "What if we don't follow those rules? What'll happen then?"

Mrs. Jeepers smiled and flashed her

green eyes. "I hope you never have to find out."

With the rules out of the way, Mrs. Jeepers started classwork. Everybody remembered Mr. Davis' warning for a little while and the morning went smoothly. Mrs. Jeepers seemed to be a pretty fun teacher. During social studies she even told the class about her home country.

Mrs. Jeepers started speaking very softly. "I come from the country of Romania." She picked up a globe and spun it to show where Romania was located.

"Jeepers doesn't sound like a Romanian name to me," Eddie said.

Mrs. Jeepers flashed her eyes in his direction. "My real name is too difficult to pronounce. I changed it when I came to America."

All the students leaned forward to hear her better. Even Eddie, who always tried to act as if he weren't paying attention, leaned on his elbows and listened.

"Romania is a small country bordered by Russia and the Black Sea. I grew up on my family's estate at the foot of the Transylvanian Alps. It was a wonderful life until . . ."

"Until what?" Liza blurted.

Mrs. Jeepers flashed her green eyes. "Until my family was forced to leave."

"Why did you have to leave?" Melody asked.

Mrs. Jeepers gently touched her brooch. "Oh, that is not important now," she said with a little half smile. Then she dismissed the class for recess.

3

The Haunted House

A group of third-graders met under the giant oak tree on the playground. The tree's branches were like a tent above them. A breeze whispered through the golden leaves.

"I think she's strange," Melody said. "Have you noticed her odd little smile?"

"I think she smiles because she's nice. And her accent is really neat!" Liza said.

"I think her accent is freaky. And what about that Romanian story?" Howie asked.

Carey nodded her head. "Why do you think her family had to leave? Do you think they're criminals?"

Melody's eyes got big. "Maybe they're jewel thieves. That's probaby where she got that huge brooch she wears. Have you noticed how she keeps rubbing it?"

Eddie reached over and pulled Melody's ponytail. "Yeah, she could even be a murderer," he snickered. "I bet she murdered all the kids in her last class!"

Howie gave Eddie a push. "Be serious! We need to decide how we're going to treat Mrs. Jeepers!"

Eddie rolled his eyes. "I think you guys need to get serious. Mrs. Jeepers is just an ordinary teacher with a strange-sounding voice. As a matter-of-fact, I think she's an old-fashioned softie!"

"What do you mean?" Melody asked. "What makes you think she's a softie?"

Eddie leaned against the rough trunk of the giant oak and looked each one of his friends in the eyes. "Didn't you notice that she never once raised her voice today? And what about those sissy rules on the board. No mean teacher would think about using rules like that. She didn't mention one thing about pushing, hitting, or spitting. Any teacher who knows what she's doing would have really laid down the law. But all she did was smile that silly grin!"

"So, what are you getting at?" Melody asked.

"It's simple," Eddie said. "We can get rid of this one like we got rid of Mrs. Deedee."

His friends looked at Eddie. Slowly, Howie started to shake his head. "I don't know, Eddie. This time you may be wrong. Mrs. Jeepers might surprise us!"

Later, on their way home, Eddie, Melody, and some of the other third-graders were walking down Delaware Boulevard.

"Yuck, somebody is moving into the Clancy estate. You couldn't get me to move in there for a million bucks!" Melody shuddered.

"It sure is creepy looking. I bet it's haunted with ghosts and vampires." Eddie pretended to bite a couple of the kids on the neck.

Melody shook her head. "I can't believe anybody would want to live there. They would have to be crazy."

The whole group jumped when a voice came from behind them. "Good afternoon, children. I see you have noticed my new home."

They all turned to see Mrs. Jeepers smiling at them.

"You mean you're going to live here?" Howie asked.

"Yes, is it not lovely? Would you like to come in and see it?" asked Mrs. Jeepers.

"Nooooo, thank you," Melody said quickly. "I mean, I have to get home to do my homework."

"Do not be silly. I did not give you any

homework today." With that, she took Eddie and Melody by their arms and gently pulled them toward the heavy wooden front door. The other kids suddenly heard their mothers calling them and ran home as fast as they could.

"It is so nice to have company. I do get lonely sometimes," Mrs. Jeepers said as she stepped out of the way of two moving men.

"Do you live by yourself, Mrs. Jeepers?" Melody asked.

Mrs. Jeepers smiled and looked at the long wooden box the men were carrying through the basement door. "Well, not exactly alone. But it is quiet most of the time."

Mrs. Jeepers pulled the reluctant pair into the front hall of the big house. A huge cobwebbed-covered chandelier hung from the high ceiling. A massive wooden staircase curved down to meet the dusty

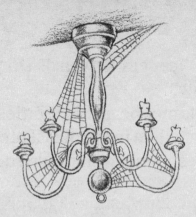

blood-red carpet. Cobwebs clung to the walls and a dusty mist filled the air.

"Is it not lovely?" Mrs. Jeepers asked. "I know it needs some work, but it really has a lot of potential."

"Er, yes, it's real nice," Melody lied.

"Would you like to see the rest of the house?" Mrs. Jeepers asked.

"We'd really like to. Maybe some other time," Eddie said quickly. "You might want to clean up or something. We'll see you tomorrow, Mrs. Jeepers." Eddie grabbed Melody's arm and pulled her out the door.

When they were safe on the other side of the street, Melody glared at Eddie.

"See! Mrs. Jeepers *is* weird! Do you believe us now?"

"All right, maybe she is a little strange for wanting to live in the old Clancy place, but that doesn't mean she's weird," Eddie said.

"I don't know, Eddie," Melody warned. "I think we'd all better watch out for Mrs. Jeepers."

4

Suspicions

Mrs. Jeepers was late for class the next morning. The students sat in their seats and anxiously listened for her footsteps.

"Maybe she quit," Liza suggested.

"Why would she quit?" Eddie asked. "She's only been here one day. She hasn't gotten the full treatment yet!"

"I don't think she quit, either," Howie whispered. "We saw her moving into the Clancy house yesterday!"

"THE CLANCY HOUSE!" several students gasped.

"That place has been empty ever since I can remember," Carey said. "I heard it was haunted!"

"Maybe a ghost ate her," Liza said. "Or maybe she was bitten by a vampire!"

"That's right!" snapped Melody. "I remember seeing the moving men carry a box into the basement yesterday."

"So?" several children chimed.

"So . . . the box was shaped long and thin — like a coffin!"

"She did say she was from Transylvania," Howie said. "And isn't that where Count Dracula lives?"

A ghostly silence filled the room as the doorknob slowly turned. Everyone snapped to attention as Mrs. Jeepers came into the room.

"Good morning, class," Mrs. Jeepers said in her strange accent. "I am sorry to be late. But I did not get much sleep last night."

Melody's eyes grew wide and Howie's mouth dropped open.

"Vampires don't sleep at night," Melody whispered to Liza.

Liza leaned over and said, "Yeah, but vampires don't wear polka dots."

Everyone looked at Mrs. Jeepers. It was true. She didn't look like a vampire today. She had on a bright pink-and-green polka-dotted dress with a bright green ribbon tied in her red hair. Her fingernails were even painted bright green. And at her neck was the green brooch.

"Perhaps we had better start with our lesson," Mrs. Jeepers suggested. "We will begin with arithmetic."

The class opened their books. Not a sound could be heard as she explained the problems and did examples on the board. Eddie looked at his friends. They were being too quiet.

Eddie wadded his math paper. The crinkling of the paper broke the silence. Several of his friends gasped as they turned to Eddie. Mrs. Jeepers didn't even flinch.

Tap-tap-tap. Eddie drummed his pencil on his desk. He glanced at his friends and noticed that some of them were moving their lips as though they were praying. Mrs. Jeepers just wrote another problem on the board.

Eddie started making goldfish noises with his mouth. The students sitting near

him sunk low in their seats, but Mrs. Jeepers didn't notice. He watched the minute hand of the clock go around three times. Still, Mrs. Jeepers ignored him. His mouth began to get dry and his jaws felt as if he had been chewing a super-big wad of bubble gum for hours. This was too much. Eddie wasn't used to being ignored, especially by a teacher.

Eddie stopped making goldfish noises and watched as Mrs. Jeepers showed the class how to work the problems for their assignment. He watched as she neatly wrote one number after another. Suddenly, an idea came to him. He held his math book high in the air. Then he let it go.

KA-BLAM! Everyone in the class jumped as the book fell to the floor with a thud. Everyone except Mrs. Jeepers.

Oh so slowly, Mrs. Jeepers ran her

fingernails down the blackboard. Cold chills escaped down Eddie's neck and back. The screeching of her fingernails on the blackboard made everyone forget about Eddie's book falling to the floor.

Turning, Mrs. Jeepers peered straight at Eddie. Calmly, and almost in a whisper, she spoke in her strange accent, "That is quite enough."

5

Hip Wiggles

Eddie couldn't believe how well the class was behaving. It really bothered him. Nobody had thrown a paper wad or spitball for days. It was as if Mrs. Jeepers had turned everyone into a goody-goody. Everyone but Eddie. Eddie hated being good. It made him sick. He was just itching to cause some trouble.

He leaned over and poked Howie in the ribs. "How about switching everybody's pencils when they're not looking?"

"Shhh! Mrs. Jeepers might hear," Howie warned.

"Well, how about . . ." Eddie started.

"Shhh!" Howie shook his head no.

Eddie turned away in disgust. Howie used to be so much fun. Now he was just another student under Mrs. Jeepers' goodness spell.

Eddie reached in front of him and pulled one of Melody's pigtails.

"Ow! Quit that," Melody whispered.

"Bet you can't make me," Eddie dared as he pulled the other pigtail.

"If you don't quit, I'll tell Mrs. Jeepers," Melody warned.

"So, see if I care," Eddie sneered, but he stopped pulling her pigtails. He tried to work on his science assignment but his heart wasn't in it.

Eddie walked up to the front of the room and wiggled his hips, making a couple of girls giggle. He stuck his already sharp pencil in the pencil sharpener. He turned the sharpener quickly and kept time by wiggling his hips. A few more people giggled, but not enough to make Eddie happy.

Eddie dropped his pencil and crawled all over the front of the classroom looking for it. He started bumping into chairs and feeling things as if he were blind. People were really watching now and some were laughing. Eddie was having a great time until he felt a hand on his shoulder.

The hand had bright green fingernails and it squeezed his shoulder, lifting him off the floor. All of a sudden, Eddie found himself looking into Mrs. Jeepers' eyes. Her green eyes flashed and then she said softly, "That is quite enough."

6

A Dare

Eddie stayed quiet for the rest of the day, and he kept an eye on Mrs. Jeepers. The rest of the class watched her, too. Something was suspicious about their new teacher, no doubt about it. Nobody could forget the way her eyes had flashed at Eddie.

At last the bell rang and Mrs. Jeepers smiled her odd little half smile. "Class is dismissed for today," she said.

Liza waved her hand in the air. "What about homework, Mrs. Jeepers? Don't you want to assign anything?"

Nobody groaned or said a word. Mrs. Jeepers looked at her class. They were sitting up straight, waiting for her reply.

"I believe we have worked enough for today. I do not think a homework assignment will be necessary. You are dismissed."

Several students sighed with relief, but nobody said a word until they had left the building.

Once outside, they gathered around the old oak tree. A few leaves drifted to the ground and crunched under the children's feet.

"That lady is definitely weird," Melody said. "I don't like the way her eyes flashed at Eddie. I think she's trouble."

Howie nodded. "I think we've definitely met our match."

"Aw, what are you guys talking about?" Eddie said. "You're acting like a bunch of sissies!"

"Then how come you acted so scared of her today?" Howie asked.

"I wasn't scared. No teacher can scare me!" Eddie shouted.

"If you weren't scared, then why did

you give up?" Melody asked.

"Yeah, and why did your face turn as white as cotton when she touched your shoulder at the pencil sharpener? How do you explain that?" Howie asked.

"I wasn't scared," Eddie sniffed. "I just didn't feel good, that's all. I think I'm probably coming down with the flu."

Melody sat down on the grass in a fit of giggles. "Eddie, you were scared, plain and simple."

Eddie's face wasn't white, now. It turned as red as an apple. "I am *not* scared of Mrs. Jeepers," he said. "And I'll be glad to prove it to you!"

His friends stopped laughing and looked long and hard at Eddie.

"Are you sure you know what you're saying, Eddie?" Liza asked softly. "We'd all understand if you want to change your mind."

"I am not a sissy like you guys and I'll

prove it. You just tell me how!"

Howie was the first one to speak. He talked slowly, choosing his words with care. "I'll tell you what, Eddie. If you find out what's in that big box in her basement, then we'll know you're not bluffing."

Everybody looked at Howie.

"Are you crazy, Howie?" Liza asked. "He'd have to sneak into her basement to find out what's in that box!"

"Exactly," Howie said. "But I think Eddie's too chicken to do it."

"Am not," Eddie snapped. "I'll find out what's in that box."

Melody looked thoughtfully at Eddie. "How will we know that Eddie really does it?"

"What's the matter, don't you trust me?" Eddie sneered.

"Of course not," Melody said. "Nobody does!"

"Well, if that's how you feel, you can come with me. Then you'll know I'm not lying! Or are you a scaredy-cat?"

Melody glared at Eddie. "I can do anything you can. We'll go tonight," she said. Then she turned and walked away.

7

The Basement

That night Eddie sneaked out of his house and met Melody in front of the Clancy place.

"Where have you been?" Melody hissed. "I've been waiting for ten minutes!"

"Well, I had to wait for my dad to sack out. Did you bring your flashlight?"

Melody patted a big bulge in her coat pocket. "It's right here. Let's go."

Eddie paused for a minute to pull his turtleneck high up on his neck. He looked at the old house. Most of the shutters were missing and every window was dark. A streetlight cast shadows on the house. Eddie was sure he saw bats circling around the light. He took a deep breath and said, "Ready when you are!"

Together, they sneaked up to the basement door. One of the glass panes in the door was cracked and another was completely broken. Eddie reached through the broken window and unlocked the door. The children froze as the door squeaked open, but the rest of the house remained deathly still.

Melody's hand trembled as she pulled out her flashlight. "Let's get this over with," she whispered. "This place gives me the creeps."

"OK," Eddie said. "You go first, you've got the flashlight."

"Here, you can have it." Melody shoved the flashlight into Eddie's chest.

Thanks a lot," Eddie said. "You're a true friend." Eddie shone the light into the dark hole leading to the basement. Cobwebs brushed their faces as they crept down the steps.

"Yuk! It smells like wet socks in here," Melody complained.

"Maybe it's a dead body," Eddie said.

"Be serious," Melody whispered.

"I am," Eddie said.

Eddie shone the light all around the dusty basement. Broken chairs and cardboard boxes littered the damp floor. The long wooden box rested in the far corner.

"There it is," Eddie whispered.

"Do you really think it's a coffin?" Melody shuddered.

"Maybe. Do you still want to go through with this?"

"Are you chickening out?" Melody asked hopefully.

"Not me! But if you want to I'll understand," Eddie said.

"I'm no chicken, Eddie," Melody said.

"Neither am I!" Eddie picked his way around the junk in the basement to the box. Melody followed silently. They stood, peering down at the box. It *was* long enough for a grown man to lie down inside.

"Do you want to open it or shall I?" Eddie asked.

"We'll do it together," Melody answered.

They placed their hands on the lid and lifted.

"Gee, this thing won't budge," Melody gasped.

"Maybe it's locked." Eddie peered at the lid, looking for a latch. "I don't see a lock."

Melody felt around the edges to see if she could find the latch. "Me neither. You don't suppose it's locked from the inside, do you?"

"Don't be so stupid. How could it be locked from the inside? That wouldn't be any good unless . . ."

"Unless someone was inside to unlock it," Melody finished for him.

Melody looked at Eddie and Eddie looked at Melody. Then they both looked at the box. Neither of them said a word. In the chilling silence they heard a thump.

"What was that?" Melody jumped and grabbed hold of Eddie's arm.

"Shhh! I don't know. But whatever it was, I didn't like it!"

"Where did it come from?" Melody asked.

"I think it came from the box," Eddie gasped.

"Let's get out of here, Eddie. Before we become vampire bait." Melody grabbed Eddie's hand and started pulling him toward the door. They dodged broken furniture, jumped over boxes, and flew up the steps. They didn't bother to close the door as they rushed into the cool night air.

Safely across the street, Melody and Eddie stopped to catch their breaths. "Look!" Eddie pointed toward the Clancy house. A light shone through an upstairs window. They dived behind a bush and watched as a series of lights flickered on. A ghostly looking woman opened the front door and peered in their direction. Was it their imagination — or did they really see something green flashing in the darkness of the night?

8

Chickening Out

"So what was in the box?" Liza asked.

"Was it a body?" Howie wondered.

"Or was it a vampire?" Carey asked.

The small group of students were huddled under the towering oak tree. It was early, at least fifteen minutes before school was to start. A nippy breeze stung their faces and a fine layer of frost covered the ground.

Eddie and Melody looked at each other nervously. They hadn't decided what to tell their friends about the night before.

"Hey, I bet they chickened out," Howie said. "Look at them, they can't say what was in the box."

"I bet they didn't even go last night," Carey said.

"We did so!" snapped Melody. "We both sneaked out of our houses and went to her house and into her basement."

"We aren't chickens!" added Eddie.

"Then what did you find?" demanded Howie.

"Well . . . the basement was really a mess," Eddie began. "It took us a while just to find the box. But when we started to open it, we heard a noise come from inside."

"Inside the box?" Howie exclaimed. "Did you open it?"

"No," Melody admitted. "But we tried. I think it was locked from the inside. And when we heard the noise, we figured we'd better get out of there!"

"That's it! Mrs. Jeepers must be a vampire. I bet that's where she sleeps at night," Carey gasped.

"I'm not so sure about that," Eddie said. "After we left, we hid in a bush. A light came on upstairs. Pretty soon Mrs. Jeepers opened the front door. If she was the vampire, then who turned on the light upstairs?"

"Besides," Howie added, "vampires don't sleep at night."

The children thought hard for a few minutes.

"Her husband must be a vampire and she takes care of him," Liza said. "Maybe he doesn't come out 'til midnight!"

"I bet her husband is Count Dracula, and he has her under his spell." Melody was so excited she was almost yelling.

"Good morning, children. What is all the excitement about?" Mrs. Jeepers had come up behind them without their even knowing it. She had on a black dress with a high collar, and a bat bracelet. And she still wore the strange green brooch.

Melody turned bright red. "Oh, nothing, Mrs. Jeepers. We were just talking about a television show we watched last night."

"Oh, I never watch television. I always have too much to do," Mrs. Jeepers said. "It is time for school to begin. We had better go inside." She started walking toward the school with Liza beside her.

"I've never seen a bat bracelet before," Liza told her. "Where'd you get it?"

"My husband gave it to me."

"Where is he?" Liza asked.

"Well, I am not exactly married anymore."

"How come?" Howie asked. "Are you divorced? My parents are divorced."

"Not exactly. My husband died," Mrs. Jeepers said.

"Oh, I'm sorry," Liza said sadly.

"It is quite all right. Sometimes I feel as if he is still with me," Mrs. Jeepers said cheerfully.

Everybody stared at Mrs. Jeepers. It seemed as if their suspicions were turning out to be true!

9

The Boss

The students filed into the room and silently took their seats. Sitting up straight, they waited for Mrs. Jeepers to begin class. She stood stiffly and looked at every student in the room.

"When I was a child in Romania, we were taught to be respectful of all others," she began. "It was a reward in itself when we pleased our elders. We only needed to be told once to keep the floors free from litter, or to keep our appearance neat."

Mrs. Jeepers paused to glance at the floor. Papers were scattered around nearly every desk. She cleared her throat once and then waited.

Some students looked uncomfortably at each other while a few others tucked in their shirts and swallowed wads of chewing gum. Then very slowly, they leaned down and scooped up trash, pencils, and erasers so that the floor was clean. Without waiting to be asked, Howie walked to the front of the room and picked up the trash can. He kept his eyes glued to the floor as he walked up and down the aisles collecting trash.

"Thank you, class, particularly Howie. I am sure I will not need to remind you again about the appearance of the room or of yourselves." Mrs. Jeepers' green eyes flashed and her brooch seemed to glow dully.

"Forgive me if I seem to be grouchy today," Mrs. Jeepers continued. "I had the unfortunate experience of having prowlers enter my home last night. They disturbed my sleep." She peered around the room, letting her green eyes rest on

Melody and Eddie for a split second. Then she blinked and smiled. "However, no harm was done and I am willing to forget the experience. I feel sure that it will never happen again! Now, please open your English books and we will begin our lesson."

Melody's hands trembled and she peeked at Eddie. He had his attention glued to his book. No one made a sound as Mrs. Jeepers began teaching the class about nouns and verbs.

The rest of the morning passed quickly. By lunchtime the third-graders had finished all their assignments and were ready for a break. In the cafeteria they quietly began to eat their lunches.

"What's wrong with you guys?" Ben asked from the next table. Ben was a fourth-grader in Mr. Powers' room. He was known for his loud voice and for the dumb jokes he told. "You're all so quiet today."

"Shhh! Mrs. Jeepers might hear you," Howie whispered.

"So what? Talking is allowed in the cafeteria. Don't tell me you're actually scared of a teacher!" Ben laughed and poked Eddie in the ribs.

Eddie washed down the rest of his peanut-butter-and-jelly sandwich with a swig of milk. "Cut it out, Ben."

"What's the matter?" Ben started to laugh. "Don't tell me you're turning into a teacher's pet!"

"No way!" Eddie hissed.

"Whatever you say, sissy," Ben teased, as both the classes stood up to empty their lunch trays.

Eddie stuck out his foot to trip Ben. He smiled when Ben's tray went crashing to the floor. "That'll teach you to call me a

sissy," Eddie snapped. He hurried to line up with the rest of his class before Ben could say anything else.

Once the third grade was back in their room, Eddie started thinking. Things had definitely gotten out of hand. He wasn't used to a teacher making him behave. This had to stop. He was determined to show Mrs. Jeepers who was boss.

10

Freeze

Eddie went into action. He knocked something off every desk he walked by, scattering papers everywhere. He stuffed a wad of bubble gum in his mouth and started popping bubbles loudly. Melody looked at him in disbelief.

"Are you crazy?" she whispered.

"I know exactly what I'm doing," Eddie said as he blew another big bubble.

Melody shrugged. "It's your funeral."

Mrs. Jeepers paid no attention to Eddie. She was too busy grading papers.

Eddie decided to give her something to notice. He slouched down in his chair and kicked his shoes off. Then he propped his feet up on the seat in front of him. Once he was comfortable, he started stretching his gum to see how long he could make it. When it finally broke, he twirled the slimy strand around his finger. Mrs. Jeepers still did not look up.

This was getting ridiculous. Then he had an inspiration. He took three giant gulps of air, put his head down, and let out a deep burp.

Howie laughed out loud but stopped when Mrs. Jeepers cleared her throat. Eddie stuffed the gum back into his mouth and with precise timing, managed to pop a bubble and burp at the same time.

A few kids around him snickered. Eddie was feeling good now. He was ready for his grand finale. He looked around to make sure everyone was watching. Then he blew the biggest bubble he'd ever blown. Just as he was ready to suck it back into his mouth, he saw Mrs. Jeepers through the filmy pink bubble.

Her eyes flashed and she gently rubbed her brooch. She held up her hand and flicked her finger in Eddie's direction. Instantly the bubble popped. Gobs of

pink, sticky gum covered Eddie's face and hair.

Mrs. Jeepers smiled her odd little half smile and then went back to grading papers. A few kids stared with their mouths hanging open. Mrs. Jeepers hadn't even moved from her desk but she had made Eddie's bubble pop!

As Eddie started pulling stringy globs from his eyebrows, he heard Howie and Melody giggling.

"What's so funny," he said, pulling gum from the tip of his ear.

Howie turned back to his work but Melody couldn't stop laughing.

"She really got you that time," Melody whispered between giggles.

"What are you talking about? It was just a coincidence!" Eddie snapped.

Melody shook her head as though she didn't believe him, then turned back to her work. Eddie finished scraping gum from his nose and chin. He decided to cut the rest of the gum from his hair when he got home. He drummed his fingers on his desk while he thought about what had happened. Things certainly had not gone the way he planned. Instead of getting Mrs. Jeepers upset, he had ended up being embarrassed in front of all his friends. This called for drastic measures.

Eddie was still trying to think of something to do when Mrs. Jeepers cleared her throat. "You have been working very nicely this afternoon. I have decided that we might play math relays for the rest of the day."

Everybody clapped their hands. Math relays were a great way to practice their multiplication tables. Two teams quickly lined up. Mrs. Jeepers stood at the front of each line and held up a flash card. Several kids were hopping up and down as they tried to think of answers while others were trying to count on their fingers.

They had gone two rounds before Eddie came up with a brainstorm. This was the perfect time to cause trouble. Even though it wasn't his turn, he yelled out the wrong answer on purpose. Mrs. Jeepers flashed her eyes at him, but continued holding up the card. The next time she showed a card, Eddie burped. His teammates stopped long enough to glare at him.

It was Carey's and Liza's turn. Carey held both her hands in front of her as if she were praying. Liza was so excited she hopped on one foot and shook her arms as if they were wet. Eddie jabbed Howie and pointed at Liza.

"Look at her," he laughed. "She looks like she's trying to fly. Watch!" Eddie started jumping and flapping his arms in the air. He bumped into several students and knocked down a chair. He didn't even notice Mrs. Jeepers.

Mrs. Jeepers rubbed her brooch until it shone bright green. "That is quite enough," she said rather sternly.

Eddie acted as though he hadn't heard a thing, but there was something about her brooch that caught his eye. He stopped jumping just to watch it. The more Mrs. Jeepers rubbed it, the more it seemed to glow. He couldn't take his eyes off it.

"We may continue our game now," Mrs. Jeepers informed the class. "We will no longer be rudely interrupted."

With serious expressions, the students turned back to Mrs. Jeepers. They no longer were excited about the game. As a matter-of-fact, it was sort of creepy because they kept having to step around Eddie. He stayed rooted in the same spot, staring at Mrs. Jeepers' green brooch for the rest of the game.

Finally, the bell rang. As the class lined up, Mrs. Jeepers walked over to Eddie. She placed her left hand on her brooch, then snapped her fingers in front of his face.

"Hey," he said loudly. "Aren't we going to play anymore?"

11

No Ordinary Teacher

The third-grade class gathered outside in their usual place — under the big oak tree.

"Did you see what Mrs. Jeepers did to Eddie?" Melody squealed.

"I couldn't believe it," Liza said. "Are you OK, Eddie?"

"What are you guys talking about? She didn't do a thing to me all day. She let me get away with murder!"

"Eddie, she hypnotized you into a frozen Popsicle and you didn't even know it!" Howie shouted.

"You guys are crazier than you look. Mrs. Jeepers is a wimp and I can prove it. Tomorrow I'll give her a day she'll never forget."

"Eddie, are you crazy?" Howie asked.

"Mrs. Jeepers is a witch or a vampire or something. There's no telling what she'll do to you if she really gets mad."

"Mad, smad. Just wait until tomorrow. Mrs. Jeepers will run out of that room faster than you can say Transylvania." Eddie turned and stomped off.

Melody looked at Howie. "You know, maybe we should do something about Mrs. Jeepers. I mean, it is definitely not normal to hypnotize a student during math class."

"I know," agreed Howie. "But who could we tell? Mr. Davis would probably laugh us right out of his office."

Melody nodded her head. "Either that or put us in a nuthouse."

"What about your parents? Would they believe you?" Howie asked.

"No, my mom would just tell me to stop exaggerating, and I'd probably get in trouble for telling lies about my teacher."

"Yeah, me too," Howie sighed. "It's crazy. Here we are trying to save our class from total destruction by a mad woman and nobody will believe us!"

"I guess we're just gonna have to depend on ourselves," Melody said.

"I just hope we'll be a match for Mrs. Jeepers," said Howie.

"Me, too," Melody said softly.

The next morning Howie and Melody were the first to meet under the big oak tree. Howie pulled out a large book from his bookbag.

"Look what I got from the public library last night." Howie held up a book called *Vampires and Witches: The True Story.*

"Did you find out anything?" Melody asked.

"I stayed up late and read the whole section on vampires. I found out what we need to do to protect ourselves if Mrs. Jeepers really is some kind of vampire," Howie said.

"What do we need to do?" Melody took the book and started flipping through it.

Howie spoke with authority. "There are a couple of things vampires can't stand. One is a cross." Howie pulled open his jacket to reveal a huge gold cross necklace that hung around his neck. "Another thing they don't like is garlic," he continued.

Melody's eyes grew wide. "Did you bring some garlic, too?"

"We didn't have any real garlic at home so I brought this." Howie held up a small plastic bottle labeled garlic salt.

"Do you think that'll work?" Melody asked.

"Well, it's worth a try. Will you go with me to sprinkle it around the classroom?" Howie asked as he gathered up his stuff.

"Me?" Melody squeaked. "Why don't we wait for somebody else to come and help?"

"Because if we wait too long, Mrs. Jeepers will be there," Howie said impatiently. "And if we don't do it today, she might turn Eddie into a frog — or hypnotize him forever!"

"I guess you're right," Melody agreed reluctantly. Eddie wasn't exactly her favorite person, but she still didn't want anything bad to happen to him.

They tiptoed into the school and held their breath as they opened the classroom door.

"Good, she's not here yet," Howie whispered. Without another word he started sprinkling the garlic salt all around the room, especially around Eddie's desk. He had used every last drop when the door to the classroom opened suddenly. In walked Mrs. Jeepers.

"Good morning, children," Mrs. Jeepers smiled. "This is quite a surprise. What are you two doing here so early?"

Howie quickly slipped the empty bottle of garlic salt into his pocket and answered. "We thought we might be able to help you with something."

Melody quickly added, "Yeah, we wanted to help you pick up paper and straighten books and stuff."

Mrs. Jeepers rubbed her brooch softly. "Why, how very thoughtful of you. You can get started right away."

Melody and Howie exchanged a look of relief and started cleaning the room.

12

Ker-choo

As soon as Eddie arrived, trouble began. "Phew, somebody stinks!" he yelled. "Who had spaghetti for breakfast?"

Howie and Melody gestured to Eddie to be quiet, but he ignored them. Instead, he skipped to the back of the room and dumped the contents of his bookbag. At least twenty paper airplanes floated to the floor. As the rest of the kids entered, Eddie took aim. Paper planes soared diz-

zily around the room and then drifted to the floor.

Mrs. Jeepers was too busy blowing her nose to notice Eddie's planes. But as soon as the class figured out what Eddie was doing, they wadded up his planes into tight balls and tossed them in the garbage.

"Hey! What are you guys doing?" Eddie complained.

Several children glared at Eddie and hissed, "Shhhh!"

They all went to their seats, sat up straight, and gave Mrs. Jeepers their full attention. But not Eddie. He took all the books off the shelves and scattered them on the floor. He didn't notice that Mrs. Jeepers had gone into a sneezing fit.

"Ker-choo, ker-choo, KER-CHOO," she wheezed. "Excuse me, class. Something seems to be making me sneeze . . . ker-choo!" Mrs. Jeepers pulled a tissue from the box on her desk and blew her nose.

Her eyes were red and tears crept from their corners.

Liza waved her hand in the air. "When I have an allergy attack my mother does major house cleaning. She says it's the dust and cat hair that makes me sneeze. Maybe I should go get the custodian."

Melody leaned over and pinched Liza. But she sat back up when she noticed Mrs. Jeepers looking her way.

"Ker-choo," Mrs. Jeepers said. Then she shook her head. "That won't be necessary, Liza. I believe I know what is making me sneeze. There's only one thing it could be. I just cannot imagine how garlic has gotten into this room."

Howie sucked in his breath real fast, while Melody started digging through the books in her desk. Neither one noticed how Mrs. Jeepers' teary eyes were glowing green.

Meanwhile, Eddie had stopped taking

the books off the shelves. He glanced at Mrs. Jeepers and watched while she blew her nose again. Her allergy was interfering with all his pranks. As far as he could tell, Mrs. Jeepers wasn't even able to see him through her tissues.

Eddie stepped over the books on the floor and headed for his desk. He pulled a few pigtails and pinched a few ears on his way. He stretched and pretended to yawn before slumping to his desk. "So are you sick or something?" he hollered. "Sick people shouldn't come to school. You're exposing us to all your cootie germs!"

Howie covered his eyes and Liza gasped. But Mrs. Jeepers acted as if she hadn't heard a thing. She turned and began to write the morning assignments on the board. She had to stop every so often to sneeze, but soon the board was full and the class got busy.

Eddie looked around him with disgust. The room was so quiet that he could hear pencils scratching on paper. The only other sound was Mrs. Jeepers' sniffles.

By lunchtime, Eddie had already sharpened all of his pencils and a few of his crayons until they were nubs. He had dumped the entire contents of his desk on the floor and kicked them halfway across the room. He had hummed, whistled, and burped until his mouth hurt. But Mrs. Jeepers had been too busy blowing her nose to pay any attention to him. As he followed the rest of the class to the cafeteria, he made his brain work double time trying to think of ways to make her notice him.

Eddie got his lunch tray and sat next to Howie and Melody. "What's wrong with everybody? Don't tell me you're turning into super-students. I've been trying all day to drive Mrs. Jeepers batty.

You guys haven't helped one bit!"

Melody sadly shook her head. "Eddie, can't you get it through your thick skull? Mrs. Jeepers is not ordinary. She's some kind of vampire or witch. If you're not careful, she just might turn you into a frog."

Eddie giggled hysterically. "You've been watching too much TV! There are no such things as vampires or witches."

"Well, if that's true, then tell me why Mrs. Jeepers can't stand the garlic I sprinkled around the room?" Howie asked. "According to a book I got at the library, vampires are repulsed by garlic!"

"Well, I think garlic is repulsive and I'm not a vampire. So that doesn't prove anything," Eddie snapped. "But I do know that this teacher has got to go. So far she's made us clean up the room, get our work done, and be quiet in class. Before you know it, she'll have us actually learning! We've got to do something about her, and fast. And if you're not going to help, I'll just have to get rid of her myself!" With that, Eddie grabbed his tray and stormed away.

Melody shook her head and pushed her tray away. "All of a sudden I'm not too hungry," she moaned.

"Me neither," agreed Howie. "But I *am* scared!"

13

I Have Had Enough

Eddie rushed into the room, ready to cause more trouble. He bumped into the custodian who was just leaving.

"Thank you for sweeping the room, Mr. Dobson. I am sure I will feel much better now," Mrs. Jeepers said.

Melody and Howie gave each other a worried look and then went to their seats. Howie leaned over to Eddie's chair to whisper, "I've got to tell you something."

"Don't bug me, I'm getting ready to bombard Mrs. Jeepers with spitballs."

"But you can't," Howie hissed. "The garlic's gone. Mrs. Jeepers is already feeling better."

It was true. Mrs. Jeepers was no longer blowing her nose or sneezing. Her nose was still a little red, but her green eyes were back to normal. But Eddie was too bent on causing trouble to notice.

He stuck a wad of paper in his mouth and got it good and soggy. With his tongue he rolled it into a small ball. Then, taking careful aim, he let it fly.

SPLAT! It landed right in the middle of Mrs. Jeepers' desk.

"Bingo!" Eddie grinned.

Mrs. Jeepers slowly plucked the spitball from her papers. Her green eyes flashed

as she calmly stood up from her chair. She started to open her mouth to speak when, SPLAT! Another spitball whizzed by her cheek and landed on the blackboard.

Eddie smiled as though he had just won the World Series. He leaned over to Howie and bragged, "See, she's a wimp. She won't do a thing."

Howie didn't answer. He was too busy staring at Mrs. Jeepers. The class was so quiet that when she started speaking in a low voice, it sounded as if she were booming.

"I have had enough."

Her green eyes flashed and her brooch glowed as she deliberately made her way to Eddie. With a trembling hand she grabbed his arm. "Come with me," Mrs. Jeepers demanded.

Eddie whimpered. "I-I-I'm s-s-sorry, Mrs.

J-J-Jeepers. I'll never do it again."

Mrs. Jeepers pulled Eddie from his desk and said *very* quietly, "I will speak with you in the hall this instant."

Everyone watched as Eddie was led into the hall. The door closed with a thud.

"What do you think she'll do to him?" Melody whispered.

"I don't know," Howie gasped. "But I'm glad it's not me!"

All the kids slowly nodded their heads. One by one the whole class started picking up stuff off the floor. While they were at it, they cleaned the blackboards. Then they sat down at their desks and hurried to finish all their work.

They all looked up when the door creaked open. Mrs. Jeepers was back to normal, but Eddie looked as white as a ghost.

* * *

The students met under the oak tree after school. Melody was the first to speak. "What'd she do to you, Eddie?"

"It must've been awful," Howie exclaimed. "You hardly said a word for the rest of the day."

Eddie shook his head, but he didn't speak.

Liza piped up, "You can tell us. Did she grow fangs and bite you on the neck?"

"Don't be stupid," Howie snapped. "She didn't bite him . . . did she?"

All eyes turned to Eddie. With a shudder, he started to speak hoarsely. "I'll only say this, you guys were right. Mrs. Jeepers is no ordinary teacher."

"Is she a vampire?" Liza asked.

Howie grabbed Eddie's arm. "C'mon, you can level with us."

But Eddie wouldn't tell them what happened. All he said was, "I know one thing. I'll never make her mad again."

For the rest of the year, Eddie kept his promise. As a matter of fact, nobody in the third grade at Bailey Elementary ever dared make Mrs. Jeepers mad. And her green brooch never glowed again, although she wore it every day.

On the last day of school, the kids met under the oak tree.

"I can't believe the year's over," Liza said.

"I can't believe we lived through it," Eddie moaned.

"But, you know," Melody said, "Mrs. Jeepers wasn't so bad."

Howie said, "She's really not *that* weird."

Melody laughed. "I can't believe we ever thought she was a vampire!"

"After all," Liza agreed, "vampires don't wear polka dots!"

Werewolves Don't Go To Summer Camp

To our parents, for keeping the werewolves away

D.D. and M.T.J.

1

The New Camp

"I'm scared," Liza whispered.

Melody rolled her brown eyes. "Camp won't be so bad."

A new summer camp had been formed close to Bailey City. All the parents thought the week-long camping program was a great idea, and practically every kid from the second and third grades at Bailey Elementary School had been signed up for the first session. They were all on a big green bus taking them to the camp.

"What's the worst thing that could happen?" Howie's freckled face peered over the seat in front of them.

Liza's eyes got wide. "I could get lost in the woods and be eaten by wild animals."

"Only if we're lucky," Eddie teased from the seat behind them.

Melody ignored him. "Don't worry, Liza, there aren't any wild animals around here. And if you get lost in the woods, I'll make everyone look for you no matter how long it takes."

"But what if we both get lost together?" Liza asked.

"Don't be stupid. I'm not going to get lost anywhere." Melody squeezed her legs together. She had needed to go to the bathroom ever since they'd left the school parking lot. There was a bathroom on the bus, but Melody didn't want to use it.

Liza tapped Melody on the arm. "I'm carsick."

"Well, don't puke on me." Eddie pulled his T-shirt over his red curly hair.

Melody felt a little sick herself, but she'd seen Liza throw up on too many school trips to ignore her. "Stick your head out the window and you'll feel better," Melody said quickly.

Liza had just poked her head out the window when she hollered, "I see the sign for the camp. We're almost there."

"Thank goodness," Melody said. She wasn't thrilled about going to camp either. But at the moment there was nothing that would make her happier than a nonmoving bathroom.

All the kids strained to read the sign as the bus pulled onto the gravel driveway. It read *Welcome to Camp Lone Wolf.*

2

Mr. Jenkins

Eddie was out the door of the bus almost before the wheels stopped moving. He never could wait for anything.

All the other kids piled out after him. But not Melody or Liza.

"Come on, Liza," Melody urged. "I've got to go."

"I'm scared," Liza whined. "I've never been here before."

"None of us have," Melody snapped. "It's a brand-new camp."

"What if the camp counselors are mean? For all we know, they could be escaped convicts!"

Melody rolled her eyes. "Well, you can sit here all day if you want, but I have to go and I'm going now!" With that she grabbed her blue Bailey School gym bag and headed for the door.

Liza sure didn't want to be alone, so she clutched her gym bag and followed Melody.

"All right, you city slickers," boomed the loudest voice they'd ever heard. "Line up against that bus and listen for your cabin assignments."

"But sir," Melody raised her hand, "I need to—"

"You need to listen. Now button up," growled the man.

Howie pulled Melody back against the bus. "Shhh. This guy means business."

"I'm gonna do some business if he doesn't hurry!" Melody said through clenched teeth.

"My name is Mr. Jenkins," the man interrupted. His voice was loud enough for their parents to hear back in Bailey City. "I'm your camp director, so if you need anything, let me know."

"I need to go to the bathroom," Melody hissed under her breath.

"Where'd they find this nut?" Howie whispered.

"He's probably a reject from the Marine Corps," Eddie said.

"Yeah, a berserk drill sergeant," snapped Melody.

Howie nodded. "He *is* wearing dog tags."

"Shhh," Liza warned. But it was too late. Mr. Jenkins turned and glared in their direction.

"No talking in the ranks," he bellowed as he scratched his black beard, causing the tags around his neck to jingle. "Anyone who doesn't want to hear their cabin assignment can sleep outside with the wolves!"

Something about Mr. Jenkins made you listen to him. He was at least six and a

half feet tall and looked like a professional football player. His brown Camp Lone Wolf T-shirt was tight across his huge chest, and the silver dog tags hung from his thick neck. He had the kind of arms that could break a kid in half like a toothpick. His blue jeans were faded to almost white, and he wore no shoes, even though it was a chilly afternoon. But the thing that the kids noticed most was his hair.

Mr. Jenkins had hair everywhere. There was enough hair on his head for three people, and his thick beard would have made five bald men happy. Even his arms were covered with a forest of black hair.

Everyone quieted down as he called out the cabin assignments. Eddie and Howie ended up together in Cabin Silver Wolf along with six other boys from Bailey City. Luckily, Melody and Liza were both put in Cabin Gray Wolf. Melody rushed ahead of the other girls and made it to the bathroom just in time.

When Melody came out of the bathroom, the other girls had already picked out their beds. The only one left was the bunk over Liza's.

"Liza, I'll trade you," Melody said lightly.

"No, I can't sleep that high. I'd get sick and throw up all over you."

"Some choice," Melody complained. "Either I sleep in the nosebleed section, or I get puked on."

After everybody settled in their cabins it was time for dinner. Mr. Jenkins was grilling hamburgers outside.

Howie and Eddie put their plates on the picnic table and sat down next to Liza and Melody.

"What's wrong with you?" Howie asked Melody.

"Twitter brain there is making me sleep on the top bunk." Melody glared at Liza.

"I'll probably fall off and break my neck!"

"But I don't like the top bunk," Liza whined. "It makes me sick to look over the edge."

"I like the top bunk," Howie told Melody. "I think it'll be fun!"

"I think it'd be more fun to go home and get out of this place," mumbled Eddie with his mouth full of cold hamburger. "Yuk! These aren't even cooked." Eddie squeezed his hamburger. Red juice oozed onto the plate, leaving a puddle.

"Ew, that looks like blood." Liza gulped.

"I can't eat raw meat!" Howie exclaimed. "I'm going to see if Mr. Jenkins will cook mine a little longer."

The rest of the kids agreed. They all carried their rare beef to where Mr. Jenkins was grilling more hamburgers.

"Excuse me," Howie said softly. "But our burgers aren't quite done."

Mr. Jenkins glanced at the juicy beef

and licked his lips. "Looks done to me,"
he said. "I like my meat rare." He grabbed
Liza's burger from her plate and took a
huge bite. Juice oozed from the corners
of his mouth and dripped down his black
beard.

"Nothing wrong with this meat," he
said, licking the juice with his tongue.

Howie, Liza, and Melody went back to their seats without saying a word. None of them felt hungry anymore. Even Eddie, who usually made a smart remark about everything, was quiet as he sat down.

"I think Mr. Jenkins is strange," Howie said.

Eddie nodded. "Anybody who eats raw meat must be part animal!"

"He's hairy enough to be an animal," Liza said.

Melody laughed. "He has more hair than a wolf in winter."

"Maybe he is a wolf." Liza giggled.

"Yeah, a werewolf," Eddie added.

"Oh, there are no such things as were-wolves," Howie said.

"Sure there are," Eddie teased. "I bet Mr. Jenkins is one and he comes out at midnight for a snack. He likes to eat raw campers, especially ones named Liza!"

"Quit it, Eddie," Melody fussed. "You're scaring Liza."

"A flea could scare her," Eddie laughed.

"It could not! Besides, werewolves aren't for real," Liza said. "Are they?"

3
The Legend

"This is creepy," Liza whispered. "It's already getting dark."

Melody sighed. "You'd think a bright day was creepy."

The counselors and campers were sitting around a huge campfire. That is, all of the counselors but one. Mr. Jenkins sat back a little from the fire. In the fading light, Melody could barely make out their camp director's Camp Lone Wolf T-shirt and his hairy face. It was hard to believe he still wasn't wearing shoes even though it was a bone-chilling night.

"What's wrong with Mr. Jenkins, anyway?" Melody asked. "Why isn't he sitting with everyone else?"

"He *is* kind of weird," Liza agreed.

"From the way he acts, you'd think he was afraid of the fire instead of the dark."

Just then Mr. Jenkins began to speak. "This is your first night at Camp Lone Wolf, and I suppose some of you might be homesick. But we'll have no crybabies at this camp." His big toothy grin sent chills up all the campers' backs.

Liza shuddered. "He sure is mean."

"Shhh," whispered Melody.

Mr. Jenkins glared at them. His eyes gleamed from the firelight. "By the end of this week you'll be experienced campers, able to take care of yourselves in the wilderness."

Eddie never did know when to be quiet. "But Mr. Jenkins, we don't need to know how to live in the wilderness. We all come from Bailey City!"

Mr. Jenkins scratched his thick black beard. "You never can tell when a little kid like you might get stranded in the

woods." Eddie didn't say another word as Mr. Jenkins continued. "There's a local legend about just such a boy who wandered away from a campfire."

"Was it at this camp?" Howie asked.

"No, it was long ago, even before Bailey City was founded. The boy's family was moving west. They were camping in this area when he strayed from the campsite. They searched for that boy for three weeks, but they never did find hide nor hair of him. He simply disappeared into thin air. Except for . . . "

"Except for what?" Liza squeaked.

Mr. Jenkins glanced at the faces around the campfire. "Well, it's probably only a coincidence, but ever since he disappeared, the howling of a lone wolf can be heard in these woods. A howling that had never been heard before."

Liza dug her fingernails into Melody's

arm. "Did the wolf eat the boy?" she asked.

Mr. Jenkins slowly shook his head. "No one knows. But on certain nights, especially when there's a full moon, that wolf can still be heard. That's how this camp got its name."

A few kids looked up nervously. The sky had suddenly darkened as heavy clouds covered the nearly full moon.

"I bet you're just trying to scare us," Eddie cried. "There aren't any wolves around here!"

Mr. Jenkins scratched his beard and stared at Eddie. "If you're so sure, why don't you sleep outside tonight? The rest of you better head for your bunk beds. Sleep well, if you can!"

One of the camp counselors covered the flames with dirt while the campers headed to their cabins.

"Are you gonna do it?" Howie asked

Eddie. "Are you going to sleep outside?"

"Naw. Mr. Jenkins is just trying to scare us," Eddie said.

"Why would a grown man try to scare a bunch of kids?" Liza asked.

"Because he's a wolf," Melody whispered. "I bet he's a werewolf!"

They all jumped as a flash of lightning streaked across the sky, and thunder rumbled in the distance.

By the time everyone arrived at their cabins they were soaking wet.

"Gee, it's really coming down in buckets," Eddie sputtered.

Howie dumped water out of his sneakers. "It's a good thing you don't have to sleep outside tonight."

"Sleeping outside doesn't scare me!" Eddie boasted.

"What about the wolf?" Howie asked.

Eddie stretched out on his bunk. "You don't believe that stupid legend, do you?"

"I don't know. Mr. Jenkins is awfully hairy. . . . He just might be a werewolf."

Eddie rolled his eyes. "There are no wolves around here. And there is no such thing as a werewolf."

"Well, if you're so sure, why don't you sleep outside like Mr. Jenkins said?"

"In this rain?" Eddie gasped. "I'd drown!"

"Then do it tomorrow night," Howie dared. "If you're really not scared, you will!"

"I'm not scared," Eddie declared. "I'll do it!"

Huge bolts of lightning cut through the night sky, and thunder boomed. Eddie and Howie both jumped as the lights flickered, then went dead.

With the lights out there wasn't much anybody could do but go to sleep. The cabin counselor lit lanterns while everybody put on their pajamas.

* * * * *

Over in Cabin Gray Wolf, the girls got ready for bed by lantern light, too. When all the girls were in their bunks, and the lanterns were turned out, the girls found out what dark really was. Melody couldn't even see her hand in front of her face until there was a flash of lightning. She was just starting to get drowsy when Liza whispered her name.

"Melody, can I sleep with you?"

"I thought you were scared of the top bunk," Melody said into the darkness.

Liza hoisted herself onto Melody's bed. "Please? I'm more scared of the dark."

"Oh, all right." Melody sighed and squeezed over to one side of the tiny bed as Liza snuggled down under the covers.

Melody was too crowded to sleep so she stared out the window beside her bed.

A lantern from another cabin cast an

eerie glow on the nearby trees. Thunder rumbled in the distance. The rain pounding on the roof nearly put her to sleep. Melody's eyes shot open just as a bolt of lightning cut through the sky. The light was so bright, she could see the hunched figure of a hairy beast dashing into the woods.

Melody grabbed Liza's arm. "Did you see that?"

"Leave me alone," Liza muttered. "I'm trying to sleep."

"Liza!" Melody cried as she shook her friend. "I saw it, I saw it!"

"Saw what?" Liza mumbled sleepily.

"The wolf," Melody whispered into the darkness. "I saw the lone wolf. And it was wearing dog tags!"

4

Dead Man's Float

"It was after the lights went out and everyone else was asleep," Melody said at breakfast the next morning. "I saw a wolf creature run into the woods."

"Aw, you were just dreaming," Eddie sneered as he crunched on some bacon.

"I really did see it," Melody insisted. "Didn't I, Liza?"

"Maybe it *was* just a dream," Liza said softly. "I didn't see anything."

"It was kind of spooky when the lights went out," Howie added. "Maybe you just imagined it."

"I did not. I really saw a wolf!" Melody looked like she was ready to cry.

"There *is* no wolf!" Eddie snapped. "And I'm gonna prove it tonight."

Melody's face grew pale as she opened her mouth to speak. But she never got the chance.

"Prove what?" growled Mr. Jenkins as he walked up behind Eddie.

The campers peered up at their camp director. He had dark circles under his eyes as if he hadn't slept all night. He still wore his Camp Lone Wolf T-shirt, faded jeans, and dog tags. His hair was tangled, and his beard seemed even bushier than yesterday.

Howie finally broke the silence. "Oh, Eddie's just kidding around. It was nothing, really."

Mr. Jenkins rubbed his beard and turned away. "Everybody into their swimsuits," he yelled.

Liza whimpered, "But I don't know how to swim."

"You don't know how to do anything," Eddie sneered.

Mr. Jenkins faced Liza. "Swimming lessons are free. Besides, you need to learn. Only the fittest survive in the wilderness! And swimming is an excellent way to stay fit." Mr. Jenkins reached out and pinched Liza's plump arm. "And it looks like you need some exercise," he added.

After changing into their bathing suits, the campers met on the dock at the lake. Mr. Jenkins was already there.

Eddie poked Howie in the arm. "Look at the hair on Mr. Jenkins."

Howie had already noticed. As a matter-of-fact, all the campers were staring at Mr. Jenkins. Black curly hair crept all the way up his arms and over his shoulders. He had more hair on his chest and back than most dogs.

"I've never seen so much hair in my life," Melody whispered. "And he's still wearing those dog tags!"

Mr. Jenkins silenced their whispers with a single look before jumping into the water. "Everybody in," he growled from the water. "You'll never learn the dead man's float standing on the dock."

Some of the campers stuck their toes in, as if they were testing their bathwater. But Eddie didn't budge.

"The water is too cold," he said just loud enough for everyone to hear. "It'll wrinkle my fingers."

"And it's way too deep," Liza added. "I might sink."

Mr. Jenkins' eyes looked like slits as he squinted into the sun. Then he started to swim to the dock. He didn't swim like most grown-ups. Instead, he kept his head high above the water.

"Look at that," Melody hissed. "He's doing the dog paddle!"

Mr. Jenkins pulled himself onto the dock in front of Eddie, Liza, Howie, and

Melody. Water dripped down his legs and formed a puddle around his feet. Mr. Jenkins licked the water from his mustache. Then, starting with his belly, he began to shake, spraying the campers with water.

Liza grabbed Melody. "He's acting just like a dog."

"Or a wolf," Melody added.

Mr. Jenkins finished shaking. He scratched his beard and looked straight at the campers. "You *will* get in, or I'll teach you the dead man's float the hard way."

"How's that?" gulped Liza.

"Get in, or you'll find out," growled Mr. Jenkins.

Liza backed away from the dripping Mr. Jenkins.

"Be careful," Howie whispered. But it was too late. Liza took one step too many and fell off the dock. She came up splashing like the Loch Ness monster, swallowing almost a gallon of lake water.

"Help me," she gasped. "I'm drowning."

Eddie didn't think twice. He jumped in to rescue her, but Liza just climbed on top of his head, pushing him underwater.

"Help!" she screamed.

Mr. Jenkins splashed into the lake beside them.

"Save me! Save me!" Liza wailed.

Mr. Jenkins scooped up Liza with a big hairy arm and held her high above the water.

Eddie popped his head above the surface and spurted out a stream of water. "Were you trying to kill me?" he screamed.

"But I was drowning," Liza sniffed.

"You moron. This water only goes up to our belly buttons!" Eddie stood up to prove his point.

Liza's face turned bright red. "Oh," was all she could say as she wiped away a tear.

Mr. Jenkins put Liza down and scratched his beard. "Now that you're already wet, you two can be the first to practice the dead man's float."

After Mr. Jenkins finished the swimming lesson, the campers dried off and changed clothes. Then they headed to the dining hall for lunch.

"I wonder what torture the hairy Mr. Jenkins has planned for us now," Eddie said with his mouth full.

Howie gulped down the last of his bologna sandwich. "Maybe he's going to give us lessons on how to yell as loud as a foghorn!"

"Maybe Mr. Jenkins isn't so bad," said Liza. "After all, he did save me."

They didn't have long to wait. "Everybody finish up your lunches and head for the softball field. Let's play ball!" Mr. Jenkins' voice boomed from the corner of the dining hall.

The other counselors headed for the door. But most of the kids took their time.

"Gee," Liza sighed. "Doesn't this guy ever rest?"

Eddie shook his head. "I doubt it. After all, he does have huge circles under his eyes!"

"Besides, werewolves don't sleep at night," Melody murmured to herself.

By the time the campers had finished playing softball, it was late in the afternoon.

"Boy, I'm beat," Liza yawned.

"Me, too," Melody said. "I'll sleep like a rock tonight!"

Howie laughed. "Too bad Eddie's going to sleep *on* a rock tonight!"

"You can't be serious," Melody gasped. "Aren't you afraid of the lone wolf?"

"Of course not," Eddie said as he wiped sweat from his forehead. "Don't worry, I'll sleep like a baby." Eddie didn't talk much during supper or around the campfire that night.

Mr. Jenkins sat in the shadows and began telling the kids about the ways of wolves. "Naming our camp after a wolf is very appropriate. Wolves work together in a pack. They're much like a family. As campers, we should learn from the wolves and work together."

"Aren't wolves mean?" asked one camper.

Mr. Jenkins' black hair swayed above his shoulders as he shook his head. "Wolves have to eat just like you and me. They only prey on animals that aren't able to keep up with others."

"You sure know a lot about wolves, Mr. Jenkins," said Liza.

"Well, you might say I've had some first-hand experience with them," he explained.

"What kind of experience?" Melody asked.

Mr. Jenkins smiled. "Let's just say I've studied wolves."

"But if wolves work together, why did you tell us the legend of the lone wolf?" Howie blurted.

Mr. Jenkins' eyeteeth gleamed when

he grinned. "Last night's story was about an unusual wolf. Perhaps an outcast."

"It could've been a werewolf," suggested Melody. "Maybe that lost boy turned into a werewolf!"

"So you believe in werewolves?" Mr. Jenkins asked. "How very interesting! People in the Middle Ages believed in werewolves, and so did some tribes of American Indians. I guess many people still do believe in them."

Eddie stood up. "I don't believe in werewolves. And I'm going to prove it!"

Mr. Jenkins looked at Eddie. "And how will you prove that?"

"By sleeping outside tonight!"

A hush fell around the campfire as all the kids at Camp Lone Wolf stared at Eddie.

Mr. Jenkins licked his lips before speaking. "Are you sure you want to do that, Eddie? It gets awfully dark out here at night."

Eddie swallowed and hesitated a moment. "I'm not afraid of the dark, and I'm not afraid of wolves because there aren't any around here. It's just a stupid legend somebody made up to scare kids. But it doesn't scare me!"

Mr. Jenkins rubbed the hair on his chin. "You're welcome to sleep outside tonight if you really want to, but make sure you sleep by the fire. . . . That'll help keep the wild animals away."

5

A Cold Night in Camp Lone Wolf

Eddie didn't really think there were any wolves within two thousand miles of Camp Lone Wolf, but he put his sleeping bag next to the fire just in case.

Howie stood close to the fire with Liza and Melody. He threw a twig on the blaze and looked at Eddie. "You don't really have to sleep out here. We all know you're not chicken. Why don't you come inside?"

"Yeah, it's cold tonight." Liza shivered in spite of her blue Bailey School jacket.

"I'm as warm as toast," Eddie said as he snuggled down into the sleeping bag.

Melody pulled the hood up on her jacket. "You'd have to be crazy to want to stay out here—especially after what I saw last night. You ought to sleep inside where you have a perfectly warm, safe bed!"

"I'm safe and warm right where I am," Eddie insisted.

Melody sighed, shaking her head. "Well, you can't say we didn't warn you!"

"It's your funeral." Howie shrugged.

Howie, Liza, and Melody turned and walked toward their cabins.

"Sweet dreams," Liza called to Eddie.

"See you in the morning," Eddie mumbled.

"I hope so," Melody whispered under her breath.

The minute they left, Eddie got colder. It was hard to believe he had been sweating earlier in the day, because now he was so chilled his bones hurt.

"This really is stupid," Eddie grumbled to himself. "There's no reason for me to suffer like this."

"Still planning on sleeping out?" Mr. Jenkins' booming voice made Eddie jump.

"Yes!" Eddie sounded more sure than he felt.

Mr. Jenkins stood a few feet from the fire. "Are you sure you're tough enough to stay out here by yourself? It gets mighty dark in these woods."

"I'm not scared," Eddie said.

Mr. Jenkins smacked his lips and looked at the sky. "The moon's almost full," he growled. "It will make the night a little lighter. But, make sure you have extra firewood—just in case."

"Just in case of what?" Eddie asked.

But Mr. Jenkins had already left. Eddie watched as he disappeared behind a clump of birch trees. The leaves rustled, and then everything became still. It was so quiet Eddie could hear the toilet flushing in Cabin Silver Wolf.

"Afraid of the dark," Eddie muttered. "Whoever heard of such garbage!"

Eddie snuggled into his sleeping bag.

He really was tired. The flames of the campfire died down as Eddie closed his eyes to sleep.

Suddenly the clinking of metal came from the forest. Eddie's eyes popped open in time to see leaves trembling on some nearby bushes.

"Who's there?" Eddie whispered hoarsely.

There was no answer.

"It must be the wind," Eddie muttered. He pulled the sleeping bag up to his chin, but kept his eyes on the bushes. He watched them for what seemed like hours.

All of a sudden, Eddie heard a loud rustling sound. In the eerie glow of the moon, Eddie could've sworn he saw a hairy beast darting through the bushes. It looked too big to be an ordinary wolf.

"Holy Toledo!" Eddie yelped. He dived inside his sleeping bag and waited to be eaten. He mumbled every prayer he knew.

"If you'll just let me live, I promise I'll never beat up on my sister again!"

Then he heard it. A howl that started softly and grew louder until it pierced the night.

"The fire!" Eddie remembered. He scrambled out of his sleeping bag and frantically searched for twigs to throw on the dying fire. His hands got tangled in vines, leaving scratch marks on his skinny arms. Eddie didn't notice because another howl echoed from the bushes. It sounded closer now!

Eddie's hands closed around a bundle of twigs and dry leaves. "This better work," he said as he threw them on the campfire.

Eddie heard another howl as he took a deep breath and blew on the leaves and twigs. But there was still no flame. He blew harder and watched as the twigs caught fire and started burning.

He kept blowing on the burning twigs until the flames jumped high in the air. "You can't get me now!" Eddie yelled into the forest. The howls changed to yelps, then died away.

"Wow! That really worked," Eddie exclaimed. "But I don't know for how long!"

He looked once more at the bushes before he dashed into Cabin Silver Wolf. "Wake up!" he screamed.

A few kids grumbled from under their covers.

"Shut up, we're trying to sleep," Howie mumbled from his bunk.

Eddie bounded up to Howie's bed.

"What d'you think you're doing? Get off of my bunk!" Howie shrieked.

Eddie grabbed Howie by the shoulders. "I heard it!"

"Heard what?" Howie asked.

"The wolf! I heard the werewolf!"

"Maybe in your dreams," Howie grumbled. He hated being woken up.

"Listen, this is for real," Eddie declared. "Didn't you hear it, too?"

"I thought you didn't believe in werewolves!" Howie laughed. Then they both heard the howl of a lone wolf in the distance.

"Now do you believe me?" Eddie said soberly.

6

No Ordinary Wolf

At breakfast the next morning Melody dipped her fork into the soggy scrambled eggs on her plate. "This looks like chicken brains."

"Brains are the least of our worries," Eddie said. "There's a werewolf stalking this camp!"

"You guys are just trying to scare us," Liza insisted. "I don't believe in werewolves."

"Then what did I see last night?" Eddie asked.

"And what did I hear?" Howie turned to Liza.

"It could have been just a regular wolf," Liza said. "After all, we are in the middle of the woods."

"It could have been," Melody said. "But

I saw it, too, and it wasn't an ordinary wolf. It looked more like part wolf and part man."

"A wolfman," Eddie whispered.

"A werewolf," Howie nodded.

"And I'm sure it was wearing dog tags," Melody said softly.

"And I heard something jingling—like dog tags." Eddie agreed.

"It's an army wolf," Liza giggled.

"Maybe," Melody said, "it's Mr. Jenkins."

They all looked at their camp director. He was wolfing down a huge stack of pancakes at a table in the front of the dining hall.

"You'd think he'd never heard of a razor," Melody grumbled. "He's still wearing the same clothes, the same dog tags, and no shoes."

"He may be a slob," Liza said, "but he's not a werewolf. Whoever heard of a werewolf in a kids' summer camp?"

"You hear about crazy people everywhere," Howie said. "Why not at summer camp?"

"It's a perfect place for victims," Melody agreed. "Look at all these defenseless kids." The dining hall was filled with sleepy-eyed campers eating their eggs or pancakes.

"Well, we're not going to be victims," Eddie pounded the table. "At least not if I can help it."

"What can you do?" Melody asked.

"I don't know," Eddie admitted.

"I think we should explore Mr. Jenkins' cabin," Howie said. "If we could just get in there, I bet we'd find something we could use."

"You mean, *inside* Mr. Jenkins' cabin?" Liza asked.

"Are you crazy?" Melody asked. "He'd kill us if he found us there."

"That's a chance we'll have to take," Eddie said. "We'll go tonight."

7

In the Wolf's Den

For the rest of the day, Eddie, Howie, Melody, and Liza avoided Mr. Jenkins like poison ivy. When he was teaching archery, they took arts and crafts. When he was in charge of canoeing, they took archery.

"I wonder if an arrow shot through the heart would kill a werewolf?" Melody asked as she missed the bull's-eye with her arrow.

"No," Eddie said. "Werewolves are killed with a silver bullet."

"How do you know?" Liza asked.

"I saw it on the late late show," Eddie said.

"Well, this isn't the movies," Howie said. "So make sure you stay away from

Mr. Jenkins until we can get into his cabin."

After archery practice it was time for dinner. Unfortunately, Mr. Jenkins decided to sit by Melody. The dog tags around his neck clinked when he plopped down on the bench. His hair was matted and his beard almost touched his plate of fried chicken. Melody couldn't help but notice that Mr. Jenkins smelled like a dirty tennis shoe.

"How's camp life?" he growled as he chewed the meat off a chicken leg.

"Uh . . . fine," Melody whispered, edging away from him.

Mr. Jenkins sucked on the meatless bone. "You better eat," Mr. Jenkins said as he cracked the bone with his teeth. "You need to fatten up. There's not enough meat on you to make a good sandwich!"

Melody pushed her plate of fried chicken away. "I guess I'm not very hungry," she whimpered.

"Can't let that food go to waste. I'm so hungry, I could eat an entire chicken — feathers and all," Mr. Jenkins said. He reached over and grabbed a drumstick from her plate.

Melody, Liza, Howie, and Eddie watched as Mr. Jenkins tore the meat from the bone. Then he gnawed on the bone until it was clean.

"Nothing like a good leg," Mr. Jenkins said as he wiped grease from his beard. "You kids better finish dinner. Your cabin counselors are getting ready to teach you how to build a campfire. It's an important skill if you want to survive in the wilderness."

Eddie spoke up. "Why don't *you* teach us?"

Mr. Jenkins scratched his beard and glared at Eddie. "I leave the campfires for others to build. I find the heat a bit uncomfortable." With that, Mr. Jenkins stalked out of the dining hall.

"Did you see how he chewed on that bone?" Melody hissed.

Eddie barely nodded. "And did you notice he's getting much hairier?"

Liza didn't say a word. She was too busy eating the rest of her food.

Mr. Jenkins was nowhere in sight while the cabin counselors taught the campers to build a fire.

"Where do you think he is?" Melody whispered to Eddie.

"I bet he's already out howling. You heard what he said about still being hungry," Eddie said.

"Maybe we better not go to his cabin," Howie whispered. "It might not be safe."

Melody shook her head. "It won't be safe for any of us if we *don't* go."

"Melody's right," Eddie said. "We'll meet back here at midnight. Be sure nobody hears you sneaking out!"

That night, after everyone else had crawled into their beds and gone to sleep, Melody and Liza sneaked out of their cabin. It wasn't long before Howie and Eddie joined them by the ashes of the campfire.

"Now remember," Howie said. "We've got to find something that will save us from werewolves."

Liza shook her head. "You guys are so silly. There aren't any werewolves."

"You might not be so sure once we see the inside of Mr. Jenkins' cabin," Melody said.

The windows in their counselor's cabin were dark as they crept up and peeked inside. Just then the howl of a wolf sounded in the distance. Liza almost jumped on top of Melody. Howie grabbed Eddie's arm.

"I knew he wouldn't be here," Eddie said. "He's the one doing the howling."

"Come on," Melody said bravely. "Let's go inside."

"We're lucky the door's not locked," Howie said as the door creaked open.

It was so dark inside they could hardly see anything. Liza pulled a small flashlight out of her jeans pocket and flashed it around.

Wolf posters hung on the rough wooden walls. The cabin was only large enough for a small dresser, a chair, and the bed.

Books were piled all over the floor. Howie picked one up and gulped.

"What is it?" Melody asked.

Howie's voice shook. "It's called *The Encyclopedia of Wolves and Wolflore.*"

"That proves it," Eddie said excitedly. "Mr. Jenkins *is* a werewolf."

"That doesn't prove anything," Liza said as she shone her light on the book. "Maybe he's just a wolf nut."

"He's a nut all right," Eddie agreed. "A werewolf nut!"

"Look," Howie interrupted. "There's a whole chapter on werewolves."

"See, Liza. They do exist," Melody said.

Howie read aloud from the book. " 'Two plants commonly used to cure werewolves are wolfsbane and mistletoe.' "

"Mistletoe!" Eddie snickered. "What're you supposed to do? Kiss 'em to death?"

"I don't know," Howie admitted. "There's a picture of wolfsbane and mistletoe right here. Let's see what it says to do with them."

But Howie didn't get a chance. Just then a wolf howl sounded right outside the cabin door.

8

A Werewolf Cure

"Turn off the flashlight," Eddie whispered.

The four campers stood in total darkness, listening. Outside the cabin, they could hear something sniffing at the door.

"It sounds like a huge animal," Liza shivered.

"With dog tags," Melody said.

There was no mistaking it. They all heard the clinking of metal—and then the doorknob began to rattle!

"Quick," Eddie whispered. "Out the window."

Howie pushed. "I can't get the window open," he gasped.

"Shhh," Melody said. "It's leaving."

And indeed, the doorknob wasn't rattling anymore, and the sniffing noise had stopped. No one said a word as they listened. Whatever had been there was gone.

"I thought we were dead meat," Eddie whispered.

"Me, too," Melody admitted. "Now do you believe there's a werewolf?" she asked Liza.

Liza nodded, her eyes wide.

"And it wears dog tags," Howie said softly.

"There's only one person I know who wears dog tags," Melody whispered.

"Mr. Jenkins," they all said together.

After they sneaked back to their cabins, none of the kids were able to sleep. They were too busy thinking about a werewolf stalking their camp. When they met in the dining hall for breakfast the next morning, they were already tired.

"We've got to get the plants that book

told us about," Eddie said as he nibbled on burned toast.

"But we don't even know what wolfsbane and mistletoe look like," Melody snapped.

"I do," Howie said softly. "I saw the pictures."

"That settles it," Eddie decided. "We're in the middle of the woods. I'm sure we can find mistletoe or wolfsbane."

"But I didn't have time to read about those plants," Howie interrupted. "We don't know what to do with them once we've found them."

"We'll just have to figure it out," Eddie said.

They gobbled down the rest of their breakfast and followed the other campers outside. When they were sure that no one was looking, they all slipped behind a cabin and into the trees.

"How hard can it be to find mistletoe

and wolfsbane?'' Eddie asked. "Tell us what it looks like, Howie.''

Howie thought for a minute and then said, "Mistletoe has white berries, and wolfsbane has big purple flowers on it."

"Great,'' Eddie rubbed his hands together excitedly. "We'll find this stuff in no time flat. Then we'll really fix Mr. Jenkins."

"You don't think it'll hurt him, do you?'' Liza asked.

"Naw," Eddie said impatiently. "It'll help him be normal again. I bet he hates being a werewolf. For one thing, he can never have a steady girlfriend if he is turning into a werewolf every time there's a full moon."

"Not unless his girlfriend is a she-wolf." Melody giggled.

"Very funny," Eddie said. "Now let's spread out and find this stuff."

Everybody glued their eyes to the ground looking for anything that had white berries or purple flowers. Howie managed to run into a tree, but nobody found any wolfsbane or mistletoe.

"I don't think we're going to find it," Liza complained. "Why don't we go back to the camp and go swimming? It's getting hot."

Melody was ready to agree with Liza when she saw something in a tree. "Look," she shouted. "I think it's mistletoe." She reached up and pulled down a big clump.

"Great," Liza smiled. "Now we can get out of here."

"Not until we find the wolfsbane," Eddie said.

Howie had been out of sight for the last

few minutes, but now he came out from behind a tree shouting, "Look, you guys, I found some wolfsbane."

"All right!" Eddie slapped Howie on the back. "Now we're ready to use this stuff on Mr. Jenkins."

"How are you going to use it?" Melody asked.

"You just leave that to me," Eddie said. "I'll take care of everything."

"Fine with me," Liza said quickly. "Just tell me the way back to camp."

"That way," Howie, Melody, and Eddie all said together. Unfortunately they all pointed in different directions.

"Very funny," Liza said. "But which way is it really?"

"Don't tell me we're lost," Melody said.

"We're not lost," Howie said confidently. "I'll show you the way." He started walking, and everyone joined in behind him. They walked a long way but nothing looked familiar.

"We've never passed this rock before," Liza whimpered.

"Now we're really lost," Eddie said as he wiped the sweat from his forehead. "I knew we should have gone my way."

"Well, if you're so smart, why don't you just show us how to get out of here?" Howie's face was red.

"I'll do just that!" Eddie started walking in another direction.

"Wait, Eddie," Melody hissed. "I think I hear something."

They all listened as a clinking sound got closer and closer.

"It's Mr. Jenkins and he's going to eat us up!" Liza cried.

"Don't worry," Eddie said as he picked up a big stick, "werewolves only eat people at night."

"I hope you're right," Liza whispered as Mr. Jenkins broke through the trees. His hairy face and arms made him look like an ape or wild dog. He wore the same clothes and still had no shoes on.

"Why are you kids away from camp?" he boomed.

"We were just out enjoying the woods," Eddie lied.

"We sort of lost our way," Liza admitted.

Mr. Jenkins growled more than he talked. "The first rule of camping is to stay on marked trails. You kids might have been lost out here for days. The wild animals would love to have you for lunch."

"That's what we were afraid of," Melody said.

Mr. Jenkins gave her a dark look and bellowed, "You kids follow me back to camp and don't go out on your own again.

If you want to explore so badly, I'll have to teach you to survive in the woods. A night hike might be the perfect time."

"A night hike?" Liza shrieked.

"Yes, a night hike would be beautiful this time of year. And the moon is full enough for us to see just about everything." Mr. Jenkins scratched hard at his beard, sniffed the air, and then picked a path through the trees. "Make sure you follow me," he growled.

"Now what are we going to do?" Melody whispered.

"We'll have to work fast," Eddie said. "We don't have any time to lose." The four campers silently followed Mr. Jenkins back to camp with their pockets full of mistletoe and wolfsbane.

9

An Unusual Treat

When they got back to camp they headed right for the dining hall. Eddie was so hungry he crammed half a peanut butter sandwich into his mouth.

"How could you think of eating at a time like this?" Melody snapped. "We need to figure out what to do with these plants."

"There'll be plenty of time after lunch for that," Eddie said with his mouth full.

But Eddie was wrong. They barely had time to finish their ice-cream sandwiches before Mr. Jenkins started shouting directions.

"Campers need to know survival skills. So this afternoon we'll go on a learning hike."

Mr. Jenkins tossed backpacks to the campers. "You need to fill your canteen with water and pick up a snack from the kitchen. Meet back here in fifteen minutes."

Melody grabbed Eddie's arm as they walked to the kitchen. "Now what're we going to do? We haven't had time to spread the wolfsbane and mistletoe!"

Eddie jerked his arm away. "Just make sure to bring it with you. I think we'll be safe as long as we carry some."

When everybody was ready, Mr. Jenkins started down the trail. Howie, Eddie, Melody, and Liza followed right behind him. Their pockets bulged with the mistletoe and wolfsbane.

"We're going to hike to a remote area today," Mr. Jenkins yelled over his shoulder. "Very few people even know where it is."

Eddie jabbed Howie in the ribs. "That

means no one will be able to find us!"

Unfortunately, Mr. Jenkins heard Eddie. "You're right. If somebody gets lost, it could be for good. So make sure you stay on the trail. That's the first rule of hiking. The second rule is always hike with a friend."

Mr. Jenkins stopped to face the campers. He scratched his beard before saying, "I expect you to pay attention. You'll need to remember everything I teach you because tomorrow we're going on a night hike." With that he turned and continued up the trail.

Liza felt like her toes were going to fall off by the time they finally stopped to rest. "Whew," she complained. "Hiking is hard."

"It's good for you," Mr. Jenkins growled, scratching his neck. "It'll help get you in shape."

"Mr. Jenkins," Melody blurted. "Where are the bathrooms?"

Mr. Jenkins grinned, showing his eye-teeth. "The bathroom is as close as the nearest tree. Just watch out for poison ivy. It's real bad this time of year."

Mr. Jenkins pointed to the vines growing near several trees.

"No, thanks," Melody said. "I'll wait."

A few kids groaned as Mr. Jenkins led them up a dirt trail. It really was beautiful, with wildflowers filling the spaces between the towering pines.

"Mr. Jenkins, I'm hungry," Liza complained.

"Tough it out a few more minutes. We're almost there."

"Where's there?" Eddie asked.

"You'll see," Mr. Jenkins said. "And when we get there, we'll all have a snack."

"I could eat two humps off a camel," Howie exclaimed.

"I'm too tired to eat," Melody complained.

"You need to eat," Mr. Jenkins boomed. "You could learn from Liza. She has some meat on her bones."

"Did you hear that?" Howie whispered to Eddie.

Eddie nodded his head. "I bet he's planning on eating us during the night hike."

"Poor Liza. He'll probably eat the fat kids first. That's why he wants us to have a snack. He's trying to get us as fat as possible." Howie trembled at the thought.

"Fat or skinny," Eddie said, "it doesn't matter. He'll just eat the fat kids first. Then he'll use us for toothpicks."

"Here we are," Mr. Jenkins called from ahead. "The prettiest spot in this forest."

Directly in front of the hikers was a

cliff as tall as the courthouse in Bailey City. A waterfall tumbled from the cliff and landed in a big, sparkling clear pool.

"Wow," Liza breathed. "This is beautiful."

"It is, isn't it?" Mr. Jenkins said in a surprisingly quiet voice. "This is one reason why I love the woods."

They all gulped down their snacks and waded in the water. Eddie splashed at everyone. By the time he was finished, no one was dry. Playing in the pool was so much fun, no one gave another thought to wolves or werewolves.

After a while, all the campers climbed onto the rocks to dry. Everyone was tired but Eddie.

"Watch this," he whispered to Howie.

Eddie picked up a black hairy spider by one of its legs, then held it close to Liza's blonde hair. Before Liza even had a chance to scream, Eddie dropped the spider. But it didn't go on Liza's hair. It landed right in the center of Mr. Jenkins' huge, outstretched hand.

Eddie gasped. He hadn't seen Mr. Jenkins walk up beside him.

"I see you've found a spider," Mr. Jenkins said.

Eddie's mouth was suddenly dry. "Yeah," was all he managed to say.

"When you live in the woods you learn to eat different things," Mr. Jenkins growled. "As a matter-of-fact, I consider spiders a delicacy. Of course, you have to know which kind won't kill you."

Eddie's eyes grew wide. "Really?"

"Sure. Would you like to eat it?" Mr. Jenkins dangled the spider in front of Eddie.

"No, thanks," Eddie said as he cringed away from the struggling spider.

"Well, if you don't mind, I will." Mr. Jenkins popped the still-wiggling creature

into his mouth and smacked his lips. "Thanks for finding the treat," he said.

Eddie stood rooted to the ground as Mr. Jenkins walked away.

"Did he eat what I think he ate?" Howie gasped.

Eddie nodded. Then, in a voice that Howie could barely hear, Eddie said, "I think we may be in BIG trouble!"

10

Planting a Cure

That night, Melody, Liza, Howie, and Eddie sneaked out of their cabins again. Their pockets were still stuffed with mistletoe and wolfsbane. In the distance, they could hear the howl of the lone wolf.

"Well, at least we know that Mr. Jenkins isn't in his cabin," Eddie whispered.

"Let's hope he stays away long enough for us to hide this stuff," Howie said.

"We better look in that book and see what it says," Melody suggested. "We want to make sure we do it right." They all nodded.

When they got to Mr. Jenkins' cabin Eddie barged right in. He didn't even bother to look in the windows.

"Quick," Liza said as she clicked on

her flashlight. "Find the book."

"I can't," Howie exclaimed. "Every-thing's been moved."

"Now what do we do?" Melody whined as a wolf's howl echoed through the woods.

"Well, we don't have time to search through all these books," Eddie said. "Let's just spread this stuff around and get out of here."

Each kid pulled out a handful of wilted leaves. Howie opened a drawer in the dresser. "How about if we put some in his clothes?"

"But he never changes his clothes," Liza said. "He's worn the same thing all week."

"He has to change his underwear," Howie said as he dumped the leaves in the drawer.

Eddie took his handful and stuffed it inside Mr. Jenkins' pillowcase. "I better put some under his mattress just to be safe," he said.

"With all his hair, he's got to have a hairbrush," Melody said.

"Here it is." Liza pointed to the dresser.

Melody took the brush and crumbled leaves into it. "Old fur face ought to get a kick out of that!" she laughed.

Only Liza still had her mistletoe left. "I don't know what to do with mine," she complained. "There're no good places left."

"Well, hurry up," Eddie said. "We don't have all night."

Just then, a howl sounded nearby.

"Yikes!" Liza cried, throwing the mistletoe in the air. Little pieces of leaves scattered throughout the room. "Let's get out of here!"

All four kids squeezed through the door at the same time and raced down the dirt path to their cabins.

"That was close," Melody gasped.

Howie nodded. "We finished just in time."

"Let's hope it works," Eddie said gravely.

11

Pussycat

The next morning Mr. Jenkins wasn't at breakfast. As a matter-of-fact, he wasn't anywhere in sight.

"Maybe he vanished like the boy in the legend," Liza whispered.

Eddie shook his head. "I bet he's just resting up for tonight."

One of the other camp counselors interrupted with an announcement. "Mr. Jenkins isn't feeling well this morning. He's suffering from an allergic reaction."

Howie poked Eddie in the ribs. "It's the wolfsbane and mistletoe," he whispered.

Eddie agreed. "If he wasn't a werewolf, he wouldn't be sick."

The camp counselor continued. "Hopefully, he will be better in time for the night hike."

"Do you mean we still have to go?" Melody asked the counselor.

"Oh, yes," the camp counselor said. "Mr. Jenkins wouldn't want to miss tonight's full moon; he would just die if he didn't get to go."

"We might die if we *do* go," Eddie mumbled.

"While you're hiking with Mr. Jenkins," the camp counselor continued, "we have to clean out the cabins."

"You mean, the other camp counselors won't be coming?" Melody gulped.

"No. Mr. Jenkins said he could handle it by himself," said the camp counselor. "So for the rest of the day, we'll take it easy. We don't want you to be too tired for tonight!"

Howie, Melody, Liza, and Eddie tried all day to think of ways to get out of going. By lunchtime they were worried sick.

"I can't eat a thing," Melody said, holding her soggy taco. "I'm too worried about tonight."

Liza bit into her taco. "You might as well eat now. It may be our last meal!"

Howie agreed. "Yeah, we'd better get some food. We may need our strength for whatever happens tonight."

"Look," Melody whispered. "It's Mr. Jenkins." She pointed to a table at the other side of the dining hall. There sat a very pale Mr. Jenkins.

"That can't be Mr. Jenkins. He isn't hairy," Eddie said, shaking his head.

"But it is," Melody insisted. "Look at the dog tags around his neck."

Mr. Jenkins hardly looked like himself. He wore his dog tags, but now he had on Nike tennis shoes and clean blue jeans. His orange T-shirt was clean, too. His hair was neatly combed and pulled back in a ponytail, and no trace of a beard was left. Indeed, it was hard to believe he'd ever been hairy. Sure, he still had hair on his arms. But even that didn't look as thick.

"Wow, that wolfsbane and mistletoe must've worked." Howie looked amazed.

Liza agreed. "It really must be powerful stuff."

"As long as he's around those plants, we don't have anything to worry about," Howie said. "We'll be safe until we go home tomorrow!"

"We don't have to worry about that night hike, now," Eddie smiled.

"You said it!" Melody agreed. "Mr. Jenkins looks more like a pussycat than a werewolf."

12

Almost Midnight

The night sky was as dark as ink, but the full moon lit the trail with an eerie, silvery glow as the campers followed Mr. Jenkins up the dirt trail.

"I've never seen anything like it," Melody said.

"Nobody can grow hair that fast," Liza agreed.

"Nobody human, that is," Eddie added.

Already, a thick black stubble covered Mr. Jenkins' face. His hair was tangled and even his arms looked hairier.

"The wolfsbane and mistletoe must not affect him when he's away from it for long!" Howie declared.

"If only we'd saved some, maybe we'd have a chance!" Melody wailed and stumbled over a root sticking up in the trail.

"Maybe we could find some more," Eddie said. "After all, we are in the woods."

"No way," Howie moaned. "Remember how long it took us to find it the first time? And that was in broad daylight."

Liza clicked on her little pocket flashlight and said softly, "I still have some left."

"What?" they all cried together.

"I saved some of my mistletoe. I thought I could keep it until Christmas." Liza pulled a very crushed clump of leaves out of the pocket of her jeans.

"Liza, you're fantastic," Eddie said, grabbing it from her hand. "Now we just have to get close to him."

Howie pointed to Mr. Jenkins, who was far ahead on the trail. "That won't be easy. He's getting hairier by the minute."

"I wonder how long it takes him to turn into a werewolf," Melody said.

"It shouldn't be long now," Howie gasped as he looked at his glow-in-the-dark watch. "It's almost midnight. And look—he's taking off his shoes!"

The four campers gasped as Mr. Jenkins untied both Nike tennis shoes and kicked them to the side of the trail.

The other campers didn't notice that Mr. Jenkins was changing in front of their very eyes. Half of the kids looked like they were ready to fall asleep, and the rest were hooting and hollering about being out in the woods so late.

"Come on," Eddie said. "It's up to us to save everybody."

Howie, Liza, Melody, and Eddie ignored the complaints and shoves of the other campers as they pushed their way to the front of the group. Finally, they were right behind Mr. Jenkins.

Eddie used all the skill of a pickpocket as he inched closer. Holding his breath, he dropped the mistletoe into Mr. Jenkins' open backpack. He didn't dare breathe until he joined his friends.

"You did it!" Howie whispered as he patted Eddie on the back.

"I just hope it isn't too late," Eddie sighed.

13

The Lone Wolf

It wasn't long before Mr. Jenkins started to scratch.

"It's working," Eddie said as he grabbed Howie's arm.

"Thank goodness," Howie cried.

Mr. Jenkins was scratching like a dog with fleas by the time they reached the top of a hill. He turned to face the kids. His eyes looked red and teary. "We'll stop here and rest," he growled.

Everybody dropped to the ground and slipped off their backpacks. Even Mr. Jenkins.

"Oh, no!" Melody exclaimed. "Mr. Jenkins took off his backpack."

"Now what are we going to do?" Liza whined.

Howie tried to stay calm. "As long as he's near the mistletoe, we should be safe."

At that moment Mr. Jenkins stood up. He scratched his beard and announced, "I'm going to scout out the trail ahead. You kids sit tight." With that he walked off into the night leaving his backpack behind.

"We're dead, now," Liza gasped. "Without the mistletoe nearby, he'll turn into a werewolf!"

"There's nothing we can do but stick together," Howie said quietly. "We better tell the rest of the kids about Mr. Jenkins. That way everyone will be prepared."

Melody, Liza, and Eddie nodded. They turned and faced the other campers.

"You're crazy," one of them said when Eddie had finished telling them about Mr. Jenkins.

"Yeah," a little girl in front agreed. "I

don't believe in werewolves. There's no such thing."

"I think you've watched too many movies," said a boy from the back.

"But haven't you noticed how hairy Mr. Jenkins is?" interrupted Melody.

"And he's allergic to plants that are used to cure werewolves," Liza added.

"So, I'm allergic to a lot of plants," a chubby girl with pigtails said. "And I'm not a werewolf."

The rest of the kids started laughing and making fun of Howie, Liza, Eddie, and Melody. They were so busy giggling they didn't notice the clinking sound coming from the trees near the trail.

Then a low growl sounded from the clump of bushes. One by one, the kids got quiet.

"What's that?" Howie whispered.

Nobody answered as the growls grew a little bit louder.

"Maybe it's just a dog," a girl in a red jacket said.

Just then, whatever was in the bushes darted back into the woods. There was enough moonlight to show the glimmer of dog tags.

"That's no dog!" Melody exclaimed. "Dogs don't run on two legs."

"And dogs aren't that big," cried Eddie.

And then they heard it. A howl that started out low. It grew louder and louder until it seemed as if the woods were filled with the cry of the lone wolf.

"It's the werewolf!" Melody yelled. "Run for your lives!"

The campers turned and fled. Even though they were scared, they remembered to stay on the trail. They didn't stop until they were safe in their cabins.

The dining hall was quiet the next morning as all the campers thoughtfully chewed on rubbery sausage. Mr. Jenkins sat at a table all by himself. The black stubble on his face was almost a full beard, and his hair looked like it had pieces of dry leaves and twigs stuck in it. His clothes were torn and dirty. He didn't say a word about the midnight hike.

The bus arrived after breakfast. All the campers dragged their blue Bailey School gym bags onto the bus and found a place to sit down. Eddie and Howie headed toward the back of the bus. Liza and Melody sat right in front of them.

"I'm sure glad camp is over," Liza said.

Several kids sitting nearby nodded.

"We're just lucky to get away before Mr. Jenkins ate us," Howie said.

"Do you *really* believe Mr. Jenkins is a werewolf?" a scrawny boy across the aisle asked.

"You have to admit," Eddie said slowly. "Mr. Jenkins is no ordinary camp director."

The kids on the bus stared at each other. "You could say that again." Melody said.

The campers peered out the window as the bus slowly began to move. There stood Mr. Jenkins. He waved and scratched his beard. Then he took a deep breath and howled the call of the lone wolf.

Leprechauns Don't Play Basketball

To Mandy, Kevin, and Damon — D.D.
To Barbara and Lee — M.T.J.

1

Mean Green Pinching Machine

Melody and Liza met on the playground under the budding oak tree. The girls always met there before school. They were so busy giggling that neither one saw Eddie sneaking up behind them. He was wearing a Kelly green T-shirt under his blue jacket, and a green baseball cap. Eddie reached around the gnarled tree trunk and pinched Melody as hard as he could.

"Ow!" screeched Melody. "Why'd you do that?"

"You're not wearing green," Eddie said. "Everybody knows that if you don't wear green on Saint Patrick's Day you get pinched. And I'm a mean green pinching machine."

"Well," Melody snapped, "for your information, I am wearing green!"

"Where?" Eddie asked

Melody pointed to her tennis shoes. Each one was tied with a bright green shoelace. "I get to pinch you back," Melody insisted as she reached out to get him.

Eddie raced across the playground and barreled into the third-grade classroom of Bailey Elementary to have some St. Patrick's Day fun. But first, he glanced around to be sure that Mrs. Jeepers wasn't in the room.

His teacher, Mrs. Jeepers, had long red hair and eyes the color of lime Kool-Aid.

She always wore a giant brooch that matched her eyes. Mrs. Jeepers didn't allow any shenanigans. If someone tried to cause trouble, she would flash her green eyes in that student's direction and rub the brooch at her neck. There was something strange about her—very strange. Some kids even thought she was a vampire. After all, she was from the Transylvanian Alps in Romania where Count Dracula had lived. She even wore a bat bracelet, which was definitely not normal for a teacher. The third-graders in Mrs. Jeepers' room didn't dare make her mad.

Luckily, Mrs. Jeepers was nowhere to be seen. Eddie sneaked up behind Carey, the teacher's pet. She always got to school early to clean the chalkboards. Just as he had suspected, there wasn't a stitch of green on her. Eddie reached out to pinch her, but he never got the chance.

"Eddie, I am surprised to see you so

early." Goose bumps ran wild all over Eddie's arms and neck when he heard Mrs. Jeepers speak in her strange accent.

Eddie and Carey both turned to face their teacher. Mrs. Jeepers stood in the door. She wore a purple skirt that touched the tops of her black pointy boots, and her brooch was pinned to the collar of her starched white shirt. She smiled at Eddie with an odd little half smile.

"I . . . I . . . I just thought I'd play a leprechaun trick," Eddie stammered.

Mrs. Jeepers stopped smiling and she rubbed the brooch at her neck. "I will not allow activities having to do with those creatures." She shook her finger at Eddie.

Eddie blinked in surprise. "But it's just for fun. And besides, there isn't really any such thing as a leprechaun."

"Wouldn't it be neat if there were some leprechauns around here?" Carey giggled.

"*No!*" Mrs. Jeepers gasped. "Where I come from leprechauns are considered worse than blood-sucking mosquitoes."

"But why?" Carey asked. "They're so cute in pictures."

"Ahh, but the true leprechaun is not as you imagine," Mrs. Jeepers whispered. "Their mischievous tricks are a nuisance the world can do without."

179

Eddie wanted to ask more about lepre-chauns, but the bell rang to start school. As the rest of the class filed in the door, Eddie couldn't help wondering why Mrs. Jeepers didn't like leprechauns.

2

Eddie Cuts Loose

Eddie slammed his math book shut and looked around the third-grade classroom. Kids were bending over their books like they were performing heart surgery. He'd been working hard all morning, too. As a matter of fact, he'd been working hard ever since Mrs. Jeepers came to Bailey Elementary. Eddie scratched his curly red hair and watched the second hand of the clock sweep around. He tapped his pencil as each second passed.

"Shhhh," Howie hissed.

Eddie stuck out his tongue at the freckled face of his best friend. But he did stop tapping his pencil when Mrs. Jeepers flashed her eyes in his direction.

Eddie felt around inside his desk for something to do. He dug through wrin-

181

kled scraps of paper stuck to old bubble-gum wads, pencils without erasers, a pile of dried glue, broken crayons, dried-up markers, old test papers with F's, Howie's missing baseball card, and a pair of scissors. Eddie hooked his fingers into the scissors. He snipped a few of the F's off his old test papers and stuck them to a wad of bubble gum. It was then that he noticed how one long strand of Liza's hair had fallen out of her ponytail. The long clump was dangling right on Eddie's desk.

Eddie glanced up at Mrs. Jeepers. Luckily, she was busy helping Carey. He grinned wickedly and inched the scissors across his desk. Very slowly, he surrounded the hair with the sharp metal scissors. One snip and the deed would be done.

Eddie squeezed like he was pulling the trigger of a gun. But something was wrong. The scissors wouldn't close. Eddie squeezed harder but it was like they were frozen. It was then that he saw a green flash in the front of the room. Eddie gulped as Mrs. Jeepers rubbed the green brooch at her neck and smiled her odd little half smile.

Caught again, Eddie thought to himself as he put away his scissors. He never could have any fun in Mrs. Jeepers' room.

But it was almost time for gym. Gym was the one time he could really cut loose. All that basketball dribbling must have turned Coach Ellison's brains to mashed potatoes because he never knew what was going on.

Finally, Mrs. Jeepers stood up from her desk. "It is time for physical education," she said in her strange Romanian accent. "Please line up."

Every time Mrs. Jeepers spoke, Eddie got goose bumps. Her accent reminded him of a Dracula movie he'd seen. Eddie joined the rest of the class in line. As soon as his teacher turned away he pinched Liza's chubby arm.

"*Ow!*" Liza screeched. She slapped her hand over her mouth just as Mrs. Jeepers turned around.

"Is there something the matter?" Mrs. Jeepers asked Liza.

"N-n-no, ma'am," Liza stuttered.

Eddie snickered as they walked down the hall. "Scaredy-cat," he whispered to Liza.

Liza did her best to ignore Eddie. Everybody did their best to ignore him. But Eddie was itching for some excitement. By the time the class had reached the bathrooms, he had managed to pinch three people, trip two, and kick another.

But that wasn't enough for Eddie. Unfortunately for Howie, the girls' bathroom door was propped open. Eddie acted fast before he missed his chance. He grabbed Howie and pushed him into the girls' bathroom. The girls giggled as Howie stumbled out.

"What's wrong with you?" Howie whispered. "Are you trying to get in trouble?"

"No," Eddie admitted slyly. "I just want to have a little Saint Patrick's Day fun."

"You'd better watch out or Mrs. Jeepers will turn you into bat bait," Howie warned. "Then you'll be sorry."

Eddie's face grew pale. One time he

made Mrs. Jeepers so mad she dragged him out in the hall. The way her green eyes flashed and the warning she hissed had made the blood drain from his face. He never admitted to anyone what had happened in the hall, but the thought of it was enough to keep him quiet, at least until he got to the gym.

3

Mr. Potato Head

In the gym a very short man wearing a red sweat suit and green high-top tennis shoes stood beside their gym teacher. The stranger was so short he only came up to the waistband of Coach Ellison's pea-green sweat suit. The little man made Coach Ellison look like the Jolly Green Giant.

"Who's the peanut?" Eddie asked Howie. "He looks like something that fell out of Santa's sleigh."

"Yeah," Howie agreed, "and I think he fell on his face."

The boys looked at the tiny man's face. He had more lines on it than watermelons had seeds.

Liza whispered, "I bet he's a million years old."

"This guy is definitely a good candidate for a face-lift." Melody giggled.

"Yes," Liza agreed. "But he has a nice smile. He reminds me of my grandpa."

"I bet your grandpa doesn't carry a marble bag." Eddie pointed to a small leather pouch hanging from the stranger's waistband. He knew it was the kind that held marbles.

Coach Ellison interrupted them. "Boys and girls, I'd like to introduce you to Mr. O'Grady. He's a teacher from Ireland."

"Top of the morning, lads and lassies." Mr. O'Grady's eyes darted from face to face.

Coach Ellison slapped Mr. O'Grady on the back. "We're very lucky to have Mr. O'Grady visiting for a few days. He'll be teaching a lesson on Irish folk dancing." With that, Coach Ellison left for the teachers' lounge.

Some of the kids groaned, but not Eddie. "This will be great," he whispered to

Howie. "A brand-new teacher to drive batty."

Howie shook his head. "Mr. O'Grady looks like he's been around the block a few times. He might not be as easy as Coach Ellison."

Eddie laughed. "How much trouble can a man the size of Mr. Potato Head be?"

Just then "Mr. Potato Head" started talking with an Irish accent. "Children, it's delighting me to be your coach and friend."

Mr. O'Grady's voice had a ring to it that sounded like birds singing on a spring morning. But Eddie wasn't bothering to listen. He didn't want to waste precious time listening to a guy who wasn't tall enough to get ice cream out of the freezer.

First, Eddie squeaked his tennis shoes on the wooden floor. It sounded like he'd eaten too many beans. Eddie giggled but no one else seemed to notice. They were too busy listening to the strange-sounding shrimp in the red sweat suit. He was talking about doing a dance. *What a sissy thing*, Eddie thought. Eddie wasn't the least bit interested so he turned his attention to Melody.

She was listening to Mr. O'Grady like he was giving the answers to tomorrow's math test. Quietly, Eddie crept up behind her and tied her green shoestrings together in a double knot. Then he stood back to watch the action.

"Now, let us be a-trying the jig," Mr. O'Grady said. All the third-graders moved to their assigned places. Melody moved, too. But her feet didn't go along.

Ker-plunk! Melody fell on the floor with a thud. "Ohhhh," she wailed as Mr. O'Grady ran up to help her.

"What has happened to this beautiful lassie?" Mr. O'Grady asked.

Melody sniffed and pointed to Eddie. "He made me fall."

"Oh, me lucky charms," Mr. O'Grady smiled. "I did not think I'd be a-finding an imp so quickly."

"He's an imp all right," Melody snarled as she untangled her shoes. "He's always causing trouble."

"Let's not be too hasty to pass judgment on him," Mr. O'Grady said. "Sometimes much can be gained by tricks."

Eddie felt goose bumps cover his arms and neck. He wasn't used to a teacher being cheerful after one of his pranks.

"Gee," Howie whispered as Mr. O'Grady helped Melody off the floor. "He doesn't get mad very easily."

"We'll see about that," Eddie snapped. "If there's one thing I know, it's how to make teachers mad."

But Howie didn't hear Eddie because Mr. O'Grady started the record player. The lilting music of fiddles and flutes filled the gym. Mr. O'Grady put his hands on his hips and started to step to the music. It wasn't long before everybody joined him. Everybody, that is, except Eddie.

4

Bowling for Dancers

Eddie watched his friends act like grass-hoppers on a trampoline. "There's no way I'm going to hop around like that," he muttered while sneaking behind the bleachers.

There, waiting for Eddie, were enough basketballs to make thirty seals happy. The balls were in two huge string bags. Eddie jerked on the strings and turned the balls loose. With only a little help from Eddie they started rolling straight for the dancers and Mr. O'Grady.

"Bowling for dancers." Eddie giggled as he waited for kids to start falling. But the balls never reached their targets. Instead, they slowed down and stopped. Eddie scratched his head. "What's going on?"

Eddie didn't notice Mr. O'Grady reaching deep into his marble bag as the balls started rolling again. Only this time, they were heading straight for Eddie.

Eddie stepped away from the rolling balls, but they were like magnets. The more he high-stepped, the more the balls bumped against his feet.

"I'm glad to see you are a-joining our happy jig." Mr. O'Grady's voice suddenly came from behind him.

Eddie jumped and banged into the bleachers. He rubbed his head and stuttered. "N-n-ooo. Dancing's for girls."

"To dance is to live," Mr. O'Grady smiled. "My people always are a-dancing. 'Tis the men that love it the most!"

Eddie rolled his eyes. "Then the men are sissies!"

The sound of Mr. O'Grady's laughter matched the music from the record player. "'Tis nothing wrong with liking a good time!"

Eddie couldn't argue with that.

Mr. O'Grady's eyes crinkled with laughter as he continued. "Dancing is one of three ways we folk have fun."

"What are the other two ways?" Eddie asked as he kicked a basketball out of his way.

Mr. O'Grady pulled open his drawstring pouch. "A little dancing and a few more gems in our pouches make us happy as a robin in spring."

Eddie stared at the sparkling stones of different colors in the pouch. "Where did you get those?" he asked.

"That's what I'm a-telling you." Mr. O'Grady laughed as he pulled out a stone the color of a cherry. He rubbed it gently with his thumb. "The folk like to collect stones from around the world."

Eddie stared at the bright gem. "Jewelry is for sissies, too," Eddie finally said. "What's the third thing you do to have fun?"

"'Tis the favorite pastime of the folk,"
Mr. O'Grady whispered. "But a thing
the monsters from Transylvania cannot
stand."

Eddie jerked to attention. "What do you
know about Transylvania?"

"I know they cannot stand the tricks of
the folk," Mr. O'Grady said.

"But Mrs. Jeepers is from the Transylvanian Alps," Eddie blurted. Then he
wished he'd kept his mouth shut because
Mr. O'Grady's face grew as red as his
sweat suit.

"This teacher of yours, would she have
hair the color of the sunrise? And be a
serious sort who allows no fun-loving
shenanigans?"

"Boy, that's for sure," Eddie agreed.

"And would she be wearing a brooch
the color of spring grass?" Mr. O'Grady
asked.

Eddie's eyes got big as he nodded.

"So she *is* here," Mr. O'Grady chuckled

as he slid the red stone into his pouch
and jerked the string tight.

Mr. O'Grady grabbed one of the basketballs and twirled away from Eddie. With-

out another word he zigzagged his way
through the dancing third-graders to the
record player. The screech of the needle
across the record brought the dancers to
a halt.

"What's the matter?" Liza asked. "Weren't we doing the dance right?"

Mr. O'Grady smiled. "You dance like butterflies in a field of daisies. But our friend Eddie seems to be a-wanting to play with basketballs instead."

All the kids glared at Eddie, who was still trying to kick away the basketballs.

"But I was having fun dancing," Liza whined.

Melody nodded her head. "Eddie ruins everything."

Mr. O'Grady bounced the ball. "Basketball is a grand way to be having fun, too. Why, back home they call me Magic O'Grady on the court. Let me be a-showing you a few tricks."

The third-graders watched Mr. O'Grady dribble the ball down the center of the court. His little pouch jingled with each step.

"Aw, that's nothing," Eddie sneered as Mr. O'Grady went by. "My kid sister could do that with her eyes closed."

Mr. O'Grady stopped in the middle of the court just long enough to reach into his little pouch.

Suddenly, the ball became an orange blur as Mr. O'Grady whizzed the ball between his legs and around his back. The kids gasped as the little man in the red suit twirled the ball on the tip of one finger. In the next second, he threw the ball all the way down the court. As the ball swished through the net without touching the rim, Mr. O'Grady danced a little jig.

"All right!" Howie clapped and poked Eddie in the ribs.

Eddie watched as the third-graders of Bailey Elementary crowded around the short gym teacher and then he shrugged. "We'll just see how long his Irish luck lasts!"

5

Green Blood

"You'd think we could at least cut out some green shamrocks," Liza complained at the lunch table.

"Maybe we will this afternoon," Melody suggested as she tore open her sandwich bag.

"No." Eddie shook his head. "Mrs. Jeepers doesn't want to have anything to do with Saint Patrick's Day. All because she hates leprechauns."

"What's to hate?" Howie asked. "They're just make-believe creatures."

"Yeah," Liza agreed. "They're cute, too."

"Not according to Mrs. Jeepers," Carey broke in.

"From listening to her, you'd think leprechauns were responsible for the black plague," Eddie said in between bites of an apple.

"She must know something about leprechauns that we don't know," Melody said.

"I'll ask my grandmother to tell me about Saint Patrick's Day and leprechauns," Howie thought out loud. "She's visiting this week and she was born in Ireland."

Melody giggled. "I bet you have green blood. You're probably part leprechaun."

"Just because somebody's from Ireland doesn't mean they're a leprechaun," Howie said. "If that was true Mr. O'Grady would be a leprechaun."

"Well, he is short," Melody pointed out.

"And he does carry a pouch," Liza said. "I bet it's full of gold."

"That's not a pouch for gold," Eddie interrupted. All his friends turned to look at him.

"How do you know?" Melody asked.

Eddie shrugged. "Because he showed me."

"What's in it?" Howie asked.

"Just a bunch of stupid stones," Eddie said as he bit into his chocolate fudge brownie. "He collects them."

Melody gasped. "He *must* be a leprechaun. He's from Ireland, he's short, and he's got a treasure. He probably has a pot of gold hidden somewhere."

"What are you talking about? There's no such thing as leprechauns." Eddie sounded more sure than he felt.

Howie shrugged. "Maybe not. But Mr. O'Grady is no regular coach. I think we better watch out," he said quietly. "Mr. O'Grady is strange. Did you notice how he never looks straight into your eyes?"

"Yeah," Melody agreed. "He looks at your nose instead."

"He may be short," Liza said. "And he may be from Ireland, but I'm pretty sure leprechauns don't play basketball."

Everyone burst out laughing, but they grew silent when Mrs. Jeepers walked over to their table.

"Did I hear the word *leprechaun*?" she demanded.

"No, ma'am," Eddie lied.

"We were just talking about the new coach," Melody told her.

Liza spoke up. "His name is Mr. O'Grady and he's from Ireland. Isn't that neat?"

Mrs. Jeepers's face went ghostly pale and her eyes flashed. "Did you say . . . Ireland?"

Liza nodded. "He loves to dance so he taught us an Irish jig. You'll really like him."

Mrs. Jeepers' green eyes flashed. "I have no desire to meet anyone from Ireland."

"But he's so much fun!" Liza said. "And he collects different kinds of stones! He even showed them to Eddie."

"Shhh," Howie hissed, but it was too late.

Mrs. Jeepers touched her brooch. "So he has found me. I did not think it would be so soon."

With that, Mrs. Jeepers hurried away from the table and out of the cafeteria.

The kids looked at each other. Eddie finally broke the silence. "What did she mean by that?"

Howie shook his head. "I'm not sure. But I think there's going to be trouble."

6

Stairway to the Emerald Isle

That afternoon the four kids met under the oak tree. "I wonder why Mrs. Jeepers acted so strange when we told her about Mr. O'Grady?" Melody asked.

"Maybe he's her long lost husband," Liza said wistfully.

"But she acted scared," Eddie reminded them.

"Maybe her long lost husband is an ax murderer," Melody giggled nervously.

"But Mrs. Jeepers said her husband was dead," Howie pointed out.

"Maybe Mr. O'Grady's with the Irish CIA," Melody suggested. "Mrs. Jeepers might be an international jewel thief."

"Maybe Mr. O'Grady really is a leprechaun," Liza said softly. "You know Mrs. Jeepers doesn't like them."

"Why don't you guys come home with me for a few minutes?" Howie suggested. "My grandmother knows all about Ireland. I'm sure she can tell us about leprechauns. She'll know why Mrs. Jeepers is afraid of them."

"I guess it'd be okay—just for a minute," Melody said.

Everyone else nodded and headed toward Howie's house. It didn't take long for the four friends to walk the three blocks. They dumped their bookbags in the front hall and found Howie's grandmother in the family room, reading the newspaper. Her curly gray hair danced around her head and her eyes sparkled like blue sapphires.

"Well, Howie." His grandmother smiled and put down her newspaper. "You look to be bringing half the school home with you."

Howie introduced Melody, Liza, and Eddie. He was barely finished when Eddie blurted, "We need to know about leprechauns."

Howie's grandmother's smile faded, but just for a moment. "So, Saint Patrick's Day has you a-wondering about the little fairy folk. 'Tis a good thing to talk about on this fine day." His grandmother's voice tinkled with the same accent as Mr. O'Grady's. "Treat yourselves to some cookies and I'll be a-telling you some leprechaun tales."

The kids helped themselves to a handful of cookies from the kitchen and then settled down to listen.

"Once upon a time in Ireland," Howie's grandmother began.

"No, Grandma," Howie interrupted. "We have to have the true story of leprechauns."

Melody nodded. "Our teacher wouldn't tell us a thing."

"Mrs. Jeepers acted very strange today," Howie explained. "She's from Ro-

mania and she won't even talk about leprechauns."

Howie's grandmother frowned. "Saints preserve us," she said quietly. "Leprechauns are a most peculiar fairy folk. Most people don't know the true history of their race."

"But they're just cute little men who wear green and hide pots of gold at the ends of rainbows," Liza said.

"Ah, truth is a rainbow doesn't lead only to a pot of gold," Howie's grandmother whispered. "A rainbow is also a leprechaun's stairway to the Emerald Isle."

"What's the Emerald Isle?" Melody asked.

"'Tis another name for Ireland," Howie's grandmother explained. "Settle back and I'll be a-telling you the true story of the wee folk."

The four kids sat on the floor and peered up at the old woman. She spoke so quietly they had to lean forward to hear.

7

The True Story of the Wee Folk

"Long ago, leprechauns could be found throughout the world," Howie's grandmother began. "The leprechaun emperor ruled the lands by possession of the stolen Fairy Stone. There are many kinds of magic stones—red, blue, and even purple. But the most powerful one of all is the Fairy Stone. It holds a strong magic, the stone does. So powerful, that the leprechauns became a nuisance with it. They traveled the world, tricking anyone they could."

"What was the stone like?" Melody asked.

"The Fairy Stone is as green as the grass underfoot and the trees overhead. And the leprechauns were proud to have it. The emperor wore it at the throat of his scarlet robe."

"Scarlet!" Eddie nearly shouted. "But that's red. Everybody knows leprechauns wear green!"

Howie's grandmother shook her head. "Not in those long-ago times. They only began to wear green when they went into hiding."

"Why did they go into hiding?" Howie asked.

"'Twas the fault of the vampires. . . ." "*The vampires!*" all four kids yelled at once.

"Aye," Howie's grandmother nodded seriously. "The vampires grew tired of the leprechauns' tricky ways. So they decided to get the Fairy Stone away from the wee folk."

"What happened?" Melody asked. "How did the vampires get the Fairy Stone from the leprechauns?"

"They were tricked!" Howie's grandmother exclaimed. "The vampires sent a spy to live in the emperor's castle. The spy gained their trust and then sneaked

into the emperor's bedroom, taking the Fairy Stone whilst he slept."

"But that's stealing!" Liza cried.

Howie's grandmother shook her head. "The truth of the matter is that the Fairy Stone rightfully belonged to the vampires. And once they got it back, the vampires banished all leprechauns to the Emerald Isle. 'Tis then that leprechauns began to wear green and to hide amongst the trees and bushes. Some say it was because of shame, and to this day most leprechauns of Ireland are too ashamed to look at you. Some say you can control a leprechaun if you get him to look in your eyes."

"But didn't the leprechauns try to get the stone back?" Eddie asked.

"Aye, and they're still a-trying to this day," Howie's grandmother said. "But 'tis only three days that the leprechauns can be a-missing from the Emerald Isle. One day for each leaflet of the shamrock. The vampires saw fit to punish them that way."

"Was it Count Dracula who got the stone back for the vampires?" Eddie asked. "Is that who the emperor trusted?"

Howie's grandmother looked at each one of them. And then she answered in a whisper, "'Twas a teacher that tricked the emperor. The teacher of his very own children!"

The children were silent as they left the room. Out on the front porch Howie whispered. "That's it!"

"What?" Eddie asked.

"Didn't you hear what my grandmother said? A vampire, who just happens to be a teacher, stole the Fairy Stone from the leprechauns."

"So?" Melody shrugged.

"So, the vampire teacher is Mrs. Jeepers," Howie explained, "and she stole the Fairy Stone. You know that weird green brooch she always wears—that's the magic stone. And I bet those stones in Mr. O'Grady's pouch are magic, too."

"You don't know that," Melody insisted. "We don't even know Mrs. Jeepers is a vampire."

"It does sort of fit together," Liza said thoughtfully.

"Of course it does." Howie nodded his head. "And that means Mr. O'Grady really is a leprechaun and he's come to get the stone back."

"That's just a fairy tale," Eddie disagreed. "It's all a bunch of blarney!"

"You won't think so if we have a leprechaun and vampire war right in the halls of Bailey Elementary," Howie said seriously. All the kids were silent as they thought about what he said.

"If that's true," Melody whispered, "we've got to do something to stop it."

"But what can we do?" Howie asked. "We're just a bunch of kids."

"Maybe we should tell our parents," Liza suggested.

"Nobody would believe us," Melody said. "They'd think we'd gone completely bonkers."

"We've got to think of something," Howie said. "Before it's too late."

"I know what I'm going to do," Eddie interrupted. "I'll prove Mr. O'Grady isn't a leprechaun!"

8

Master Trickster

"I've got it," Eddie said the next morning as Howie, Melody, and Liza met under the oak tree.

"Got what," Melody giggled, "chicken pox?"

"You should get a job with the circus, you're so funny," Eddie snapped.

"Go on," Howie urged, "what were you going to say?"

"I know how to prove Mr. O'Grady isn't a leprechaun!" Eddie said.

"How?" Liza asked.

"If he's a leprechaun, like you think, he'll be able to outtrick me," Eddie explained as he grabbed his bookbag and headed inside.

"Wait!" Melody yelled. "It could be dangerous to make a leprechaun mad!"

But Eddie didn't listen to his friends as they followed him into the school.

"You don't know who you're dealing with," Howie pleaded.

"Mr. Potato Head doesn't know who *he's* dealing with," Eddie snapped as he hung up his jacket in the hallway. "But he'll find out during gym class."

Melody, Liza, and Howie tried to talk to Eddie during class, but Mrs. Jeepers flashed her eyes to silence them. For once, Eddie didn't mind.

Just before gym, Eddie raised his hand. "Yes?" Mrs. Jeepers asked in her strange accent.

"May I please be excused?" Eddie asked as politely as he knew how.

Mrs. Jeepers raised her eyebrows and looked hard at him. But then she slowly nodded her head. "You must hurry. We will be ready to leave for physical education in less than five minutes."

Eddie nodded and rushed out of the

room. He got back just as the class was lining up. Nobody noticed that Eddie was wearing his jacket as he slipped into line between Howie and Liza.

"What are you going to do?" Liza asked with concern.

Eddie patted his bulging jacket pocket. "I'm going to prove that I'm the master trickster!"

The third-graders entered the gym. Mr. O'Grady was standing on the other side of the gym bouncing a basketball. He looked from face to face, but he didn't look in anybody's eyes. "Top of the morning to you," he called. "Won't you be a-joining me for a little game of basketball?"

Eddie beat everybody to the other side of the gym and stood in front of Mr. O'Grady. The little man glanced at Eddie's raised hand.

"What would you be a-wanting?" Mr. O'Grady asked.

Eddie looked at Howie and grinned before he answered Mr. O'Grady. "Can we dance again today?"

"I thought you would rather be a-shooting hoops." Mr. O'Grady glanced around the gym. "But 'twould be a pleasure to be teaching you another Irish jig."

"No," Eddie interrupted. "I want to teach you a dance of *ours*."

Mr. O'Grady touched the leather pouch hanging from his waistband and gently tugged on the string. "And what might you be a-calling this dance?"

Eddie grinned as he pulled a small jar out of his pocket. "It's called the Honey Bee Waltz," he yelled as he unscrewed the lid. "And it's guaranteed to keep you hopping!" And with that, Eddie lightly rolled the jar toward Mr. O'Grady's feet.

Carey was the first to scream. "Bees! Watch out for the bees!" And then she ran out the door.

The jar broke and honey bees swarmed out and onto Mr. O'Grady's bright red sweat suit.

"Watch out," Liza screamed. "They'll sting you!"

But Mr. O'Grady didn't seem upset at all. Instead he reached into his leather pouch and pulled out the small red stone. One by one, the bees flew away and out the open gym window.

"Wow!" Howie yelled. "How did you do that?"

"To be sure," Mr. O'Grady chuckled, "'twas just a bit of Irish luck. But since you like to dance so much, we'll have another jig tomorrow."

Howie jabbed Eddie. "So much for your Honey Bee Waltz!"

"Shut up," Eddie muttered as he plopped onto the bleachers. It was then that Eddie found out—not all of the honey bees had left.

"Oww!" Eddie jumped up and grabbed

his behind. "I've been stung!"

"Look, everyone," Melody yelled, "Eddie's doing the Honey Bee Waltz."

All the kids laughed as Eddie raced out of the gym.

9

Eddie's War

Eddie wasn't surprised when Principal Davis called him to the office after school. Principal Davis looked like Humpty Dumpty with glasses as he frowned at Eddie.

"Sit down, young man," he said gruffly.

"Do I have to?" Eddie whined.

Principal Davis almost cracked a smile. "Bees are dangerous. They're nothing to play around with."

"I know," Eddie muttered.

"I don't want to catch you misbehaving again," Principal Davis continued. "Let this be a lesson to you. Tricks will get you in the end."

Eddie rubbed his bee sting. "I know," he said again as he left Principal Davis' office.

His friends were waiting for him under the oak tree.

"Now do you believe us?" Melody said. "Mr. O'Grady is the leprechaun after Mrs. Jeepers' Fairy Stone."

"Maybe we should just let him take it," Eddie grumbled.

"No!" Liza shouted. "Mr. O'Grady might hurt Mrs. Jeepers."

Howie shook his head. "Besides, if Mr.

O'Grady got the stone, the world as we know it would end. Leprechauns would be running all over the place tricking people."

"Eddie wouldn't care," Melody told them. "He's always playing tricks anyway."

"He'd never get a chance to play anymore tricks," Howie said. "The leprechauns would take care of that."

Eddie rubbed his sore spot. "You may have a point. We have to do something."

"But what?" Melody cried.

"I have an idea," Howie said quietly. "We have to do what my grandmother said. We've got to make him look us in the eyes. Then he'll do whatever we say."

"How?" Liza squeaked. "Mr. O'Grady doesn't ever look straight at us."

Eddie interrupted. "There's only one way. We have to trick the trickster."

His three friends were quiet.

"How?" Melody finally asked. "You saw what he did when you tried to trick him this morning."

"Gather round," Eddie said, "and I'll tell you."

Liza's eyes grew big as Eddie whispered the plan. "Do you think it'll work?" she asked.

"It's got to," Howie said.

Melody gulped. "All right. Let's do it!"

10

Up to Their Eyeballs in Trouble

The next morning the four friends huddled under the oak tree. "It has to be today," Howie insisted. "Grandma said leprechauns can only leave the Emerald Isle for three days, and this is Mr. O'Grady's third day."

Liza interrupted. "Let's all just leave him alone and let him go back to Ireland."

"We can't," Melody explained. "Mr. O'Grady is bound to make his move to steal the Fairy Stone today."

"We have to stop him before he has the chance," Howie added.

Eddie nodded. "I'll do it today—during gym."

"What will we do until then?" Liza asked.

"Just be normal," Eddie suggested as they went into the room.

But Mrs. Jeepers was not her normal self. Her red hair hung limply around her face, and dark circles were underneath her dull green eyes. Her white blouse was wrinkled and she wasn't wearing her bat bracelet. Even her green brooch seemed to have lost its shine, and she didn't smile her odd little half smile when she said, "Hello, children."

The rest of the morning was strange, too. Mrs. Jeepers jumped at every little noise and her eyes kept darting toward the darkened hallway.

"Mrs. Jeepers seems nervous," Liza whispered.

"I think she's scared," Melody said softly.

"You'd be scared, too," Howie added, "if the future of the world was pinned to your shirt."

Nobody said a word when Mrs. Jeepers

forgot to give the spelling test. Eddie worried that she would forget about gym, too. He almost wished she would, but at 10:30 Mrs. Jeepers sighed and slumped at her desk. "Boys and girls, it is time for physical education. You may walk by yourselves to the gymnasium. I will come for you at the end of the class period."

Then she put her head down on her desk and was quiet.

"I think she's sleeping," Melody said as they tiptoed out of the room.

"I don't like seeing Mrs. Jeepers this way," Liza said softly.

"I'd like it," Eddie admitted, "if it wasn't so weird."

Melody stopped at the gym door. "I'm afraid to go inside."

"We have to," Eddie said.

Howie nodded. "Grandma said the way to capture a leprechaun is to stare at him without blinking. It's the only magic that controls him. Once Eddie has captured him, he'll have to do whatever we say."

"But what if you blink?" Liza worried.

"I don't want to think about that," Eddie shuddered.

"But if you do outstare him, you can get his bag of jewels, *and* make him leave," Howie pointed out.

"You're right. It's now or never." Eddie

gulped and rubbed his eyes with his knuckles before he followed his friends into the gym. Mr. O'Grady was waiting on the other side of the gym by the record player.

Eddie didn't waste any time. He marched right up to Mr. O'Grady and tugged on his red sleeve.

"There's something in my eye," Eddie whined.

Mr. O'Grady turned away and laughed. "To be sure, 'tis nothing but your eyeball."

"Ha, ha," Eddie said without a smile. "But I'm serious, it really hurts. You have to look at it."

Mr. O'Grady shooed Eddie away. "Don't be a-troubling me. I have a dance to be a-teaching." Then he turned on the record player and started dancing to the Irish tune.

Howie nudged Eddie in the back. "Keep trying."

Eddie stepped in front of Mr. O'Grady. "I'll be your partner," he said. But Mr. O'Grady leapt away. Eddie spent the entire gym time chasing his teacher around the hopping third-graders. Eddie was almost ready to give up when he ran smack dab into Mr. O'Grady as he was doing a twirl.

Eddie hopped up and tried to look into Mr. O'Grady's eyes. But Mr. O'Grady was not to be tricked. He reached into his little pouch and sidestepped Eddie.

"Watch out!" Melody squealed. "He has a magic stone."

Eddie jumped back and joined his three friends.

"Why might you be a-thinking I have magic?" Mr. O'Grady asked softly.

"We know who you are," Eddie blurted, "and we know why you're here."

"We're going to stop you," Howie added.

Mr. O'Grady pulled out the small red jewel from his pouch. "'Tis foolish to be a-thinking you can stop me!"

11

Swing Your Partner

Melody gasped when the door swung open and Mrs. Jeepers stepped into the gym.

"We've got to do something!" Melody gasped.

But it was too late. Mr. O'Grady dashed to the door and grabbed Mrs. Jeepers' hands. He started to twirl her around the gym, keeping time to the music.

"Look!" Carey squealed. "Mrs. Jeepers is dancing with Mr. O'Grady." The rest of the kids pointed and laughed. Everybody, that is, except Howie, Liza, Melody, and Eddie. They stared as Mr. O'Grady spun Mrs. Jeepers faster and faster around the gym. Her black shoes flew off the floor, and her long red hair was swept back.

"He's going too fast," Liza cried as she headed for the dancing teachers. "Mrs. Jeepers can't reach her brooch!"

"He's going to snatch it!" Howie warned.

"Not if I can help it," Eddie yelled, following Liza. Just as Mr. O'Grady reached for the sparkling brooch, Eddie dived and grabbed the little man's ankle. Mr. O'Grady went crashing to the floor. Without thinking, Liza plopped on his chest. Mr. O'Grady gasped—and looked straight at the little girl holding him down. Liza stared back at the blue eyes of the wrinkled little man.

"Don't look away!" Howie shouted. "Whatever you do, don't blink!"

Liza took a slow breath, but she kept her eyes on Mr. O'Grady.

"It's working," Melody said from behind her. "He can't take his eyes away."

"Tell him now," Howie added.

Liza nodded. "It's not that we don't like

you, it's just that Mrs. Jeepers was here first. I'm not going to stop staring until you promise to leave her alone—and leave Bailey Elementary."

"So, that's the way it 'tis." Mr. O'Grady winced.

Mrs. Jeepers towered over Mr. O'Grady—and Liza. Her green eyes flashed and she gently rubbed the green brooch at her throat. The stone seemed to glow as she spoke. "The children are correct. A school is not the proper place for your shenanigans." Mrs. Jeepers reached down to help Liza to her feet. Liza glanced at her teacher's outstretched hand.

As soon as Liza looked away, Mr. O'Grady scrambled up. A slow grin spread across his wrinkled face. "The lively jig wasn't meant to be a-causing harm. We folk must dance to live!"

Mrs. Jeepers's eyes flashed at the little man, and then she walked away. The

class fell into line behind her as she left the gym.

Liza squeezed in behind Melody, Howie, and Eddie. "I'm sorry," she whispered. "I didn't mean to look away."

"That's all right," Melody said. "Besides, maybe you stared at him long enough. After all, he was looking at you when you told him to leave."

"I just hope you're right," Howie said softly.

12

The End of the Rainbow

It started to sprinkle shortly before lunch and angry storm clouds dumped sheets of rain during math. Mrs. Jeepers didn't mention her strange dance in gym that morning, but she did seem more cheerful.

The rain slowed to a sprinkle during science, and by the time the bell rang to end the school day, the sun was trying to peep through the clouds. Melody, Liza, Eddie, and Howie stood under the oak tree. Big drops fell from the branches and plopped on their heads.

"Look!" Melody pointed. "A rainbow." Liza, Howie, and Eddie looked to see a full rainbow arching across the sky.

"It's beautiful," Liza said. "I wonder if it really does lead to the Emerald Isle."

"We'll know tomorrow," Howie said, "if Mr. O'Grady is gone."

When Mrs. Jeepers greeted the children the next morning she looked like her regular self. She wore black pointy boots, a black skirt, a starched white lace collar, and her bat bracelet. And at her neck was the sparkling green brooch. Her hair was swept back in a proper ponytail and she smiled her odd little half smile. "Good morning, children. Did you get to see the lovely rainbow yesterday?"

"Yes, it was the biggest rainbow I've ever seen," Melody said.

The rainbow seemed to put everyone in a good mood. Everyone, that is, except Coach Ellison. He nearly growled when the kids got to the gym. "I don't know what you did to Mr. O'Grady, but whatever it was, you made him leave. He left me a note saying he wanted to go back home where it was safe!"

"All right!" Howie slapped Eddie on the back. "We did it!"

"I guess we showed him who the master tricksters are," Eddie bragged.

Liza smiled. "I guess Bailey Elementary isn't big enough for a vampire *and* a leprechaun."

Melody giggled. "I don't think Bailey Elementary is big enough for a leprechaun and *us*!"

Ghosts
Don't Eat
Potato Chips

For three great brothers:
Randall J. Thornton
Frank L. Gibson
David W. Gibson

1

Great-aunt Mathilda

"Aw, Grandma," Eddie whined. "Why do I have to go? Great-aunt Mathilda doesn't even like me."

Eddie's grandmother sighed. "Because Mathilda is my sister, and families take care of each other."

"That old bat never did anything for us," Eddie mumbled.

Eddie's grandmother thumped him on the head. "That's not the point! She's been by herself since Uncle Jasper died. Now she's sick and needs our help. All you have to do is take her meals to her. You and Howie can take her lunch on your way to the playground."

Eddie pulled a baseball cap over his curly red hair and grabbed the dish off the kitchen counter. He didn't complain

to his grandmother again, but he slammed the door extra hard on his way out.

His best friend, Howie, was waiting for him at the street corner. "What's that?" Howie asked.

"It's a sick casserole for my Great-aunt Mathilda."

"Don't you mean it's a great casserole for your sick aunt?" Howie asked.

Eddie snickered. "You don't know my grandmother's cooking!"

Howie laughed and pulled out a crushed

bag of potato chips from his shirt pocket. "You want some garlic chips?"

"No! Those chips are worse than my grandmother's cooking!" Eddie said. "You should get the kind I like."

The two boys headed down a side street with Howie crunching away. In just a few minutes they stood in front of Aunt Mathilda's house.

The branches of a huge weeping willow tree dragged the ground beside the fence. The rusty iron gate squeaked open. Eddie and Howie looked at the big house without saying a word. Dark windows stared down at them as they walked up the crumbling steps to the door.

"This house looks like a reject from an old horror movie," Howie whispered.

Eddie nodded. "It's definitely ready for a wrecking ball."

Howie crunched nervously on his potato chips. "Let's hurry up, this place is creepy!"

Eddie lifted the rusting door knocker and then let it fall with a thud. A window on the second floor creaked open, and a gray-haired woman looked out. "Who's at my door?"

"It's us," Eddie yelled. "Grandma sent your lunch."

Aunt Mathilda wrinkled her nose like she'd just sucked a lemon. "Well, hurry and bring it to me. And shut the door behind you!" Then she slammed the window so hard, it rattled.

Eddie pushed the door open. A musty smell hit them like an ocean wave.

"Phew. It smells like something died in here. Hasn't your Aunt Mathilda ever heard of air fresheners?" Howie asked.

"Old people don't care when things stink," Eddie said.

"Quit that whispering and bring me my lunch," Aunt Mathilda said from her bedroom. "An old lady could die of starvation before getting fed by you."

"I'd like to feed her a thing or two," Eddie muttered. "Only it wouldn't be supper!"

The two kids stepped around a pile of yellowed newspapers and started up the creaking steps. Eddie's shoelaces slapped the faded carpet, and the boys sidestepped a broken chair in the upstairs hall. Aunt Mathilda's room was at the end of the hall on the second floor.

Aunt Mathilda was sitting up in bed with a box of tissues by her side. Wadded-up tissues were scattered on the floor. Wisps of gray hair hung around her face like spiderwebs, and her wrinkled skin was the color of old pears. She looked like she had been through World War Two instead of the flu. She pointed a bony finger at Eddie. "I remember you. You're the mean one!"

Eddie shrugged. "It must run in the family."

"Hummph," Aunt Mathilda grunted. "Who's that with you? I don't know him."

Howie choked on a potato chip. "I'm Eddie's friend, Howie. Would you like some chips?" He held out the crumpled bag.

"That's the garlic kind my Jasper always ate. It's probably what killed him."

"Who's Jasper?" Howie whispered as he stuffed the bag into his shirt pocket.

"My dead uncle," Eddie whispered back. Then, before Aunt Mathilda could say anything else, Eddie shoved the dish at her. "Grandma said to ask if you needed anything else."

Aunt Mathilda nodded. "As long as you're here, you can water the garden."

As they walked down the steps, Eddie and Howie heard Aunt Mathilda blowing her nose.

"I never knew you had a crazy aunt," Howie said.

"She's not half as crazy as Uncle Jasper was," Eddie said as he pushed open the back door. "We're just lucky he's not around anymore!"

2

Weed Soup

"I can't believe she calls this a garden," Eddie said, shaking his head. "It's just a bunch of weeds."

"I bet your Aunt Mathilda uses it to make weed soup." Howie laughed as he helped drag a garden hose between the gnarled trees.

"Crabgrass salad, too," Eddie giggled as he tried to turn on the water. "Something's wrong with this faucet."

"Let me try," Howie said, dropping his bag of potato chips on an old picnic table.

"No. If I can't get it, you sure can't." Eddie didn't get a chance to try again because Aunt Mathilda's screech interrupted them.

"Did you expect me to eat this with my

fingers?" she yelled from the window. "Bring me a fork and a glass of water."

Eddie shoved the hose at Howie. "You'll have to water the garden while I go water Aunt Mathilda."

Howie looked at the old house as his friend disappeared inside. Several windows were broken, and wood was nailed over the empty spaces. The attic window was so high, Howie had to tilt his head back to see it.

What Howie saw made him freeze. Someone was staring down from the attic window. Howie rubbed his eyes and looked again. No one was there.

"That's strange," Howie muttered.

"You're strange," Eddie said as he came out the back door. "If you don't watch out a bird will get you in the eye."

Howie ignored Eddie's remark. "Were you just in the attic?"

Eddie grabbed the hose from Howie. "I don't even know how to get to the attic of this joint."

"Does anyone else live here?" Howie asked.

"Just my crazy aunt." Eddie tried to twist the water spigot. "Why do you care?"

"Maybe we'd better call the police because I just saw someone in the attic." Howie pointed to the small window at the top of the house.

Eddie stared at the window for a few minutes and then laughed. "Don't be silly, it was just a shadow from those big trees."

Howie looked at the window again. But he didn't see anything because Eddie finally got the hose on and squirted Howie right in the face.

"Cut it out," Howie yelled.

Eddie laughed. "I thought you might like to cool off."

Howie backed away from the weed patch. "If you don't quit it, I'm going to the playground without you."

"Okay, I'll stop if you'll wait for me." As Eddie squirted the plants, Howie went to get his potato chips. Instead, he found an empty chip bag. "Who said you could eat all my chips?"

"I told you, I hate garlic chips," Eddie said.

Howie looked under the old picnic table and gulped. "Eddie, come here."

Eddie dropped the hose and walked over to the picnic table. "What do you want?" he asked.

Howie pointed. "Look under there."

Eddie shook his head, but he glanced

under the table. "So, you spilled your chips. What's the big deal?"

Howie banged his hand on the table. "Look, Eddie. Really look. This is important."

"Okay, okay. Keep your eyeballs glued on." Eddie looked again. "Hey, the chips are letters. A . . . T . . . T . . . I . . . C. What's that spell?"

"ATTIC!" Howie yelled at Eddie. "Somebody spelled out attic."

Eddie shrugged. "It's just a coincidence. Either that or Aunt Mathilda has smart ants in her yard." With that, Eddie stepped on the chips and smashed them to tiny pieces.

Howie looked back up at the attic window. It was still empty. Maybe it had been a shadow. But what if it hadn't?

3

Smarty-Pants

Eddie caught up with Howie at the oak tree on the playground. The giant tree made a perfect Saturday morning meeting place for the kids from Bailey Elementary School. Two other third-graders, Liza and Melody, were waiting for them.

Liza giggled and pushed back her blonde hair. "What happened to you?"

"It looks like you've been slimed by the Loch Ness Monster," Melody said.

Howie squeezed his T-shirt and water oozed into his tennis shoe. "Hosehead tried to squirt me into the next county."

"I was just trying to cool you off," Eddie told him. "After all, you were so hot you were seeing things."

"What's he talking about?" Melody asked.

Howie shook his wet head and splattered water on his friends. "I saw someone looking out his crazy aunt's window."

"He also saw potato chips so smart they could win a spelling bee." Eddie laughed.

Howie's face turned red. "Maybe the chips were a coincidence, but there really was somebody in the attic."

"It was probably Eddie's aunt," Melody told Howie.

"No, she's sick in bed," Howie said. "*And* she lives all by herself."

Liza touched Eddie on his shoulder. "I didn't know your sweet aunt was sick."

"There's nothing sweet about that old bat," Eddie snickered.

"Eddie! You shouldn't talk about sick people like that," Liza said.

"You guys are missing the point," Howie interrupted. "What if there really is somebody hiding up in that attic?"

"No one's up there except in your loony imagination," Eddie laughed. "I told you, it was just the tree's shadow."

"It couldn't be a shadow," Melody told them.

"How do you know that, Miss Smarty-Pants?" Eddie asked. "You weren't there."

"It's been cloudy all day," Melody snapped. "You can't have shadows without sun!"

Howie pointed a finger at Eddie. "She's right."

"Maybe you better call the police," Liza said.

"Police don't chase shadows." Eddie laughed.

"But there could be a crazy lunatic just waiting for the chance to rob your aunt," said Howie.

Eddie shook his head. "Nobody would want to rob my aunt. She's so poor she can't even afford to fix up her house."

"Still, wouldn't you feel terrible if something happened to your aunt and you didn't help her?" Liza asked.

Howie nodded. "At least tell her."

"But we just got here," Eddie snapped. "We'll tell her later."

"Stop thinking about yourself," Liza said. "You better warn her now before something awful happens."

"Something awful *has* happened," Eddie said. "I listened to my silly friends. If you goody-goodies are so worried about Aunt Mathilda, you can go with me. Meet me at her house at seven o'clock when I take supper to her. And don't be late."

His friends watched Eddie stomp away from the tree toward some boys playing softball. "Are you sure there was someone at that window?" Melody asked Howie.

"I know what I saw," Howie said slowly. "And it was no shadow."

4

The Legend

At seven o'clock, Eddie, Howie, Liza, and Melody stared up at the attic window. Liza's eyes were big and round. "You didn't tell me your aunt lives in a haunted house."

"You're as bad as Howie," Eddie told her. "Next, you'll be seeing things, too."

"Don't you know the legend behind this house?" Liza asked. "Three years ago, weird things started happening at all hours of the night. Strange lights and funny noises came from the attic."

"What kind of noises?" Melody asked.

"Ghostly footsteps," Liza said seriously, "and whistling."

"That's all stupid nonsense," Eddie interrupted.

"It is not," Liza snapped. "My dad told

me that ghosts can't rest if something they did during their lives is causing loved ones to suffer. They're doomed to wander until someone rights the wrong for them."

Eddie shook his head and pushed open the squeaky gate. "Then you'll never rest because you're always making me suffer."

"But maybe that's what Howie saw," Liza said firmly.

"What?" Melody asked.

"A ghost," Liza whispered.

"And maybe your head is full of Rice Krispies!" Eddie muttered to himself as he headed up the sidewalk. "My aunt may be crazy," Eddie told them on the porch, "but she's no ghost."

"How can you be sure?" Melody asked.

"Because you have to be dead to be a ghost, and Great-aunt Mathilda is too mean to die," Eddie joked as he banged on the front door.

Just like before, the second floor window creaked open and Aunt Mathilda peered down at them. "Quit that racket. How's a sick woman supposed to get any rest with you pounding on the door?"

Eddie held up his grandmother's casserole dish. "Should I just throw this in the trash?"

"What? And let me starve?" Aunt Mathilda snapped. "Bring it up here and don't be all day about it."

"I told you she was crazy," Howie whispered to Liza as they went in the house.

"She's not crazy," Liza said. "She's just cranky because she doesn't feel well."

"Then she hasn't felt well since 1942," Eddie said as he led them to his aunt's bedroom.

Aunt Mathilda was still in bed. Her covers looked like a warthog had been rooting in them, and the mound of used tissues on the floor had grown a foot. Aunt Mathilda reached out her hands for

the casserole dish and fork. "How many kids does it take to bring an old woman dinner?"

Liza smiled. "My name is Liza, and this is Melody. It's nice to meet you."

"Hummph," Aunt Mathilda said as she dug into her dinner.

"We came to tell you something," Melody added. But she never got the chance because Aunt Mathilda took a big bite of casserole and spit it out all over the bed.

"I can't eat this. It's as cold as a park bench in February. You'll have to heat it up in the oven."

"We'd be happy to," Liza chirped as she picked up the cold dish. Her three friends followed her out of the room.

Aunt Mathilda called after them, "Come back up here while it's heating so I can keep an eye on you."

The kids hurried to the kitchen. "I've got better things to do than play nursemaid to an old grouch," Eddie complained.

"Now, Eddie. You shouldn't talk about your great-aunt that way. It won't take long to heat this up, then we can tell her about the attic," Liza said.

"How do you work this stove anyway?" Melody asked.

"Do I look like Betty Crocker? I've never used an oven in my life," Eddie admitted.

"Me neither," Howie said.

Eddie twirled the knob. "My grandmother does it all the time so it can't be that hard."

Liza stuck the casserole in the oven, and they went back upstairs. They were in the upstairs hall when they heard it.

THUMP.

"Listen," Howie hissed. The four kids stood in the middle of the dusty hallway. "It sounds like something fell over in the attic."

THUMP. THUMP. THUMP.

"It sounds like footsteps to me," Melody whispered. "Somebody *is* up there."

"Or else it's the ghost," Liza gulped as she started backing down the hall.

Melody grabbed Liza's arm. "We've got to warn Aunt Mathilda."

"Calm down," Eddie laughed. "It's probably just rats."

"I've never heard rats whistle," Howie said hoarsely as a high-pitched melody floated down from above.

5

Up in Smoke

"Did you hear that?" Liza asked as they burst into the bedroom.

Aunt Mathilda was busy shuffling a deck of cards like a professional card-shark. "Hear what?" she asked.

"It sounds like someone is in the attic," Melody told her. "We heard footsteps and whistling."

Aunt Mathilda shrugged. "There're always creaks in an old house like this."

"But this afternoon I saw a face in the attic window," Howie said. "Maybe we should take a look around upstairs — just to be sure."

"Hummph. Nobody's going up in that attic," Aunt Mathilda said firmly. "Jasper was the only one who ever went up there.

274

It's been three years since he died and that creaky floor's probably not safe anymore."

"Are you sure it's just old floorboards?" Liza asked.

"Of course," Aunt Mathilda snapped. "Now, I've had enough of your silly talk. I want to play cards."

The four kids looked at each other and shrugged. If Aunt Mathilda wasn't worried, maybe they shouldn't be either. Liza clapped her hands. "Oh, I just love to play Go Fish."

"Fish!" Aunt Mathilda bellowed. "I was thinking more about poker."

"Now, you're talking." Eddie smiled.

The kids stared because Aunt Mathilda dealt the cards with the speed of a machine gun. It wasn't long before the five of them were playing Black Jack and Three-card Monte.

"How'd an old lady like you learn to be such a good poker player?" Melody asked

after Aunt Mathilda had won another game.

"That's one good thing about being old! I know a lot more than little snots like you." Aunt Mathilda laughed.

Liza giggled along with her. Eddie even laughed as he grabbed the cards to deal a new game.

Howie sniffed the air. "Do you smell something funny?"

"The casserole," Melody gasped.

"You're burning down my house," Aunt Mathilda screamed as the kids rushed out of the room.

The kitchen was filled with so much smoke that none of the kids noticed the dark shadow by the refrigerator.

"Turn off the oven," Eddie hollered, grabbing a potholder.

Melody reached for the dial and froze. "It *is* off!"

"Right, this burned all by itself," Eddie snapped, opening the oven door. Black smoke billowed out and Liza coughed. Eddie dropped the crispy casserole into the kitchen sink.

"Oh, no," Melody choked when she saw the black mess.

"There's no way your Aunt Mathilda will eat this," Howie said, holding his nose.

Liza took an old dish towel and started fanning the smoke. "We can't let her starve to death."

Aunt Mathilda screamed from the top of the stairs, "What're you ruffians trying to do? Cook me alive?"

Eddie looked at Liza. "Maybe we *should* let her starve."

"I like your aunt. After all, she did teach us to play poker," Melody said.

"We've got to tell her what happened," Howie said.

"Tell me what?" Aunt Mathilda snapped as she shuffled into the kitchen.

Liza reached out for Aunt Mathilda's arm. "You shouldn't be out of bed!"

"I couldn't let you barbecue me," Aunt Mathilda coughed. "I suppose you've ruined my supper," she said.

"Well," Eddie stammered. "It did get a little well done."

"Smells to me like it burned to kingdom come," Aunt Mathilda wheezed as she pulled an ancient black coin purse from her robe pocket. "Eddie, you'll have to clean this up. And open the windows to let all that smoke out! The rest of you can get my supper. I guess I'll have to pay for it. You kids must think I'm made of money."

Aunt Mathilda dug into the coin purse with her long bony fingers. Slowly, she pulled out several crumpled bills.

"I'd better give you money to buy something. If I don't you'll eat mine before you get back here."

"We wouldn't do that," Liza insisted.

"Hummph," Aunt Mathilda snorted. "Make sure you don't. Hurry to that fast food joint around the corner."

"You mean Burger Doodle?" Melody asked.

Aunt Mathilda nodded. "That's the one. Jasper loved their Double Onion Doodle Burgers and those garlic chips. Pick me up some and get something for yourselves."

"We'll be glad to get your dinner," Liza said. "But you'd better get back to bed before you start coughing again!"

"Hummph," Aunt Mathilda said as she left the room. "Just don't take all day to do it."

Eddie walked with his friends to the front door. "Will you clean up the kitchen for me?" Eddie said to Melody.

"She's your aunt," Melody smiled as she opened the door. "You clean it up. But we'll bring you back a Doodlegum Shake."

"Bring me three," Eddie ordered.

"Quit being so greedy," Liza told him.

"Well, make it fast or she'll have us running errands all night."

"She's not that bad," Liza said.

"My aunt is as rotten as those Double Onion Doodle Burgers," Eddie said. "Aunt Mathilda and Uncle Jasper are the only people I've ever known who actually ate them."

Melody giggled. "But those Doodlegum Shakes are the best in town."

"And I like the garlic chips," Howie yelled as he started running. "Last one there is a slimy Doodle Burger."

Eddie watched his friends race down the street. He closed the door and went back to the kitchen. When he got there, the casserole dish was already sparkling clean and the windows were wide open.

6

Double Onion Doodle Burgers and Garlic Potato Chips

Howie opened a new bag of garlic chips as the three kids opened the rusty gate in front of Aunt Mathilda's house. "Phew. Those Double Onion Doodle Burgers stink."

Melody held up the greasy paper bag. "You're right, you can smell these three miles away."

Liza held her nose and ran away from the burgers. "Get those away from me!"

But Melody couldn't resist teasing Liza a little bit. She chased her around the house.

Howie was still in the front yard munching his chips when he heard Melody

scream. When he got to the backyard, Melody was face down on the ground. "What happened?" he asked.

Melody lifted her face out of the grass. "I tripped over a stupid tree root," she said.

Howie grabbed an arm to pull her up. "Are you okay?"

"I'm all right." Melody sat up. "But I'm afraid these Doodle Burgers are squished.

They're flatter than a rattlesnake run over by a two-ton semi-truck."

"We'll have to fluff them up a little," Liza said.

"They're hamburgers," Melody said, "not pillows."

They didn't see the dark shadow as Howie picked up the smashed bag and headed inside.

"If anybody can fix these burgers, I can," he said as he dumped the garlic chips on the kitchen table. Then he put the burgers onto a cracked plate and patted them with his hands.

"Maybe she won't notice," Liza suggested.

"If you ask me," Howie told them with a grin, "they look better than they usually do."

"What's taking you guys so long?" Eddie asked as he clomped down the stairs. "Aunt Mathilda is starving, and I'm tired of getting beat at poker. By the way, you really had me tricked. I just can't figure out when you did it."

"What are you talking about?" Howie asked.

"When you cleaned up the casserole catastrophe," Eddie said.

His three friends glanced at each other. "We didn't touch that mess," Melody said slowly.

"Well, if you didn't clean it up, and I didn't clean it up, then who did?" Eddie asked as he turned and grabbed the plate off the counter. "Hey! Who bit the burger?"

His three friends stared at the half-eaten burger. "Not me," they all said at once.

"Look! Someone's been eating the garlic chips, too," Melody said.

"And they're all over the floor," Liza said. "What will we tell Aunt Mathilda?"

"No problem," Eddie said. "We'll just

put them back on the plate. Aunt Mathilda will never know."

The four kids picked up the chips that were scattered on the kitchen floor. "There's more out in the hall," Melody said.

"It's a garlic chip trail," Howie said quietly.

The trail led them to an open door at the top of the stairs. A cold draft made Liza shiver. "That must be the attic. It's as if someone's trying to lead us up there."

"With potato chips?" Eddie laughed.

"How did the door get opened?" Melody whispered. "I'm sure it wasn't open before."

Eddie didn't have time to answer.

"I'm going to call the police if you don't bring me some food. I'm about to pass out from hunger up here," Aunt Mathilda screamed from her room.

"She sounds to me like she has plenty

of strength left," Eddie muttered. He closed the attic door and stomped into Aunt Mathilda's room with his three friends following.

Aunt Mathilda grabbed the plate and started wolfing down a slimy Doodle Burger. Grease from the burger oozed down her bony fingers.

"That's so disgusting," Melody whispered.

"At least she didn't notice they were squished," Liza whispered back.

But Howie did notice something — a picture on Great-aunt Mathilda's nightstand.

"Look at the man in that picture," Howie said softly to Eddie. "That's the man in the attic window."

Eddie looked at the picture. "Don't be silly. That's my uncle Jasper. And he's dead."

7

Uncle Jasper?

"It's true," Howie told his friends. "The man in the window looks just like Uncle Jasper. He was even wearing the same hat." The four kids were under the oak tree. Thick storm clouds hung low in the sky.

"What a strange coincidence," Melody said.

"What's really weird is that Jasper liked Doodle Burgers," Liza pointed out. "And somebody took a bite out of one of ours."

"And someone nibbled on my garlic potato chips," Howie added.

Eddie laughed. "And my aunt thought only Uncle Jasper liked garlic chips and Doodle Burgers."

"If I didn't know better," Liza said, "I'd

say Jasper *is* a ghost, and he's living in the attic!"

Her three friends stared at her for a second before they burst into a fit of giggles.

"And Aunt Mathilda's really Joan of Arc," Eddie snickered.

Liza got mad. "This is nothing to laugh about."

"You have to admit," Melody said slowly, "it is sort of spooky."

Howie nodded. "After all, somebody did spell out the word 'attic' with my garlic chips."

"Big deal," Eddie said. "It doesn't take a college degree to spell."

"Well, explain the trail of garlic chips leading to the attic, and the foot-steps we heard up there," Melody demanded.

Eddie fell on the ground laughing. "You guys have sawdust for brains. You've been reading too many ghost stories."

"Ghosts are white and float through walls," Howie added.

"Yeah," Eddie laughed. "And they definitely don't eat potato chips."

Melody put her hands on her hips. "If you're so sure, you'll go up in the attic and prove there's no ghost."

"But Aunt Mathilda said the attic's not safe," Liza said.

"Nothing can stop me from going up there," Eddie bragged. "Not even Aunt Mathilda."

8

Ghost Hunt

"Why do we have to go tonight?" Melody asked. The four kids were standing in front of Aunt Mathilda's house. The wind was blowing the leaves, causing a strange rustling sound.

"We have to go when she's asleep, don't we?" Eddie swung the gate open. "We're here. Let's get it over with."

"I can't believe we're actually going ghost hunting," Howie shivered.

"There *is* no ghost," Eddie said.

"Ghost, or no ghost, I don't see anything," Melody whispered. "How do we find a ghost?"

"Let's call him," Liza suggested.

"He's not a dog," Eddie snapped.

"How else do you plan on finding him?" Liza asked.

Eddie shrugged his shoulders. Then they all started whispering into the darkness. "Jasper! Jasper!"

"Shhh," Melody hissed. "I think I hear something."

They all strained to hear.

"Ohhhh. . .Ohhhh."

"My gosh," Liza screeched. "It's Uncle Jasper's ghost."

"It's coming from inside the house," Melody whispered.

"Ohhhh . . . Ohhhh," they heard again.

"We've got to go in there and find what's making that noise," Eddie said bravely.

"Not me," Liza and Melody said together.

"What about Aunt Mathilda? We can't leave her in there with a ghost!" Howie reminded them.

"You're right," Liza nodded. "Poor Aunt Mathilda. She's probably scared to death."

"My Great-aunt Mathilda isn't scared of anything," Eddie bragged.

"Ohhhh . . . Ohhhh," they heard again.

"Come on," Eddie said, and he pushed open the front door. His three friends followed closely behind him.

"Your aunt should lock her door," Melody said. "Anybody could just walk in."

"Anybody just did," Eddie snickered.

"Listen," Liza whispered. "I hear whistling."

"It's just the wind blowing through cracks," Eddie said.

"I've never heard the wind whistle 'Yankee Doodle' before," Howie muttered.

It was true. Someone was whistling the lively tune. "It must be Aunt Mathilda," Eddie said. But when they reached her bedroom, the entire house was deathly still.

"Aunt Mathilda?" Eddie whispered outside her bedroom door. "It's me, Eddie. Are you okay?"

There was no answer.

"Maybe she's asleep," Howie said.

"Maybe the ghost got her," Liza suggested.

"You better go in and check on her," Melody said quietly.

"I'm not going in there," Eddie said. "She could be in her underwear!"

"She's your aunt." Liza shook her finger at Eddie. "You have to go in there."

"You're all chickens," Eddie accused.

"Am not," Melody snapped.

Eddie grabbed Melody's arm. "Then prove it! Go with me."

Slowly, he turned the knob, and the door groaned open.

9

Yankee Doodle

Aunt Mathilda was sprawled across the rumpled bed. Her face was white as a ghost.

"Is she d-d-dead?" Melody whispered.

Before Eddie could answer Aunt Mathilda slowly opened her bloodshot eyes. "Of course I'm not dead," she wheezed.

Eddie snickered, "She's too mean to die!"

Liza touched his arm and said softly, "She looks pretty sick to me."

Aunt Mathilda grabbed her chest as she broke into a coughing fit. "Jasper," Aunt Mathilda gasped. "Get in here. I need you."

"She's finally done it," Eddie said. "She's gone completely bonkers."

"Jasper," Aunt Mathilda called again.

Eddie touched his aunt's hand. "Uncle Jasper is dead and gone."

"No, he's not." Aunt Mathilda coughed and pointed to the door. "I hear him."

"All I hear is somebody whistling 'Yankee Doodle'," Howie said softly.

Aunt Mathilda nodded. "That's him! That's my Jasper!"

"I think she's had one Double Onion Doodle Burger too many," Eddie mumbled.

"I think you need to call her doctor," Melody said.

"NO!" Aunt Mathilda screamed. "I can't afford a doctor."

"You have to go to the doctor," Eddie said. "You're sick. Besides, Grandma says you have plenty of money."

Aunt Mathilda shook her head. "That's why you have to get Jasper. He has all the money. If you won't get him, then I will." Aunt Mathilda threw back the covers and stuck out her skinny legs.

"She's delirious," Eddie told his friends. "I'm calling 911. You keep her in bed."

His friends could hear Eddie racing down the steps to the phone in the kitchen. Melody grabbed Aunt Mathilda around her waist and wrestled her back into bed. "Hurry," Melody screamed as she threw the covers back on the old woman. "Your aunt is burning up with fever. We've got to get her to the hospital."

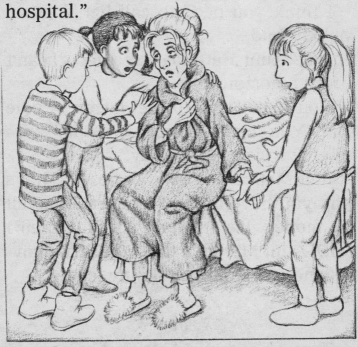

"But I'm too poor to go to the hospital," Aunt Mathilda wailed. It took all the kids to hold Aunt Mathilda in bed until the ambulance came.

"Put me down," she yelled as the medics slid her into the back of the ambulance. "I don't want to go to the hospital."

When the tall medic patted her hand, Aunt Mathilda tried to bite him. "I said, put me down," she told him. "I can't afford hospitals."

As he climbed into the ambulance, the medic glanced at Eddie. "Your aunt will be fine. But she better be able to find a way to pay. Hospitals aren't cheap, you know."

Eddie looked him in the eye. "Don't worry. She'll pay."

Lightning cracked the sky, and thunder rumbled in the distance as the ambulance sped away.

"But Aunt Mathilda doesn't have money," Liza said softly.

"Maybe Eddie's grandmother will help," Howie said. "Right now, we better make sure all the windows are closed, and get home. I think those clouds are ready to dump a billion gallons of rain."

Melody shivered and looked at the thick clouds. Then she glanced at the old house. "Look!" she screamed. "Look in the attic window."

Her three friends glanced up just in time to see the shadow of a man wearing a hat.

"Oh my gosh," Liza screamed. "It's the ghost!"

10

Ghost in the Attic

"It's not a ghost," Eddie said. "And I'll prove it." He didn't give his friends a chance to argue. Fat raindrops splattered to the ground as they followed Eddie inside. The rain fell harder and a bolt of lightning struck close to the house. A gust of wind billowed the curtains and the front door slammed shut. Melody jumped and Liza screamed. Then the lights went dead.

Howie tried a switch. "There's no electricity."

"Yes, there is," Eddie said quietly. "There's a light coming from upstairs." It was true. A single light cast an eerie glow on the steps.

"Let's get out of here," Liza whined.

Melody ran to the door and pulled on

the knob. "The door's stuck. We're trapped inside."

"There's only one way to go," Eddie told his friends. Slowly, he started up the steps with his three friends close behind. The light led them to the open attic door. The kids swatted away clinging cobwebs as they climbed the attic steps.

Melody grabbed Howie's arm. "Do you hear that?" All four kids stopped to listen. CREAK. CREAK. CREAK.

"It's just the wind," Eddie told her as they continued up the stairs. When they reached the top, he pointed to the ceiling.

A single light hung down in the middle of the attic. It slowly swayed, back and forth, casting eerie shadows all around.

"Why are there lights in the attic and nowhere else?" Melody whispered.

"It's the ghost," Liza whimpered as thunder rattled the attic window.

The four kids gulped and stared at the swinging light. Below the light sat an old trunk. "Hey, that looks like the box we saw in our teacher's basement," Eddie remembered.

"It does," Melody agreed. "We thought it was a vampire's coffin."

Eddie nodded to the trunk. "This one's long enough for a vampire, too. Do you think Aunt Mathilda keeps vampires in her attic?"

"Shhh. Listen," Melody hissed. "I think I *do* hear something inside the trunk."

Liza squealed and covered her eyes. "It is a vampire and it's coming to get us!"

"It sounds to me more like whistling," Howie whispered.

"It's just the wind in this old attic," Eddie said. "C'mon. Let's find out what's in the trunk."

"Go ahead," Melody said.

Eddie shook his head. "You look."

"I'm not going to open it," Melody said.

"We'll count to three and look together,"

Howie interrupted. "One . . . two . . . THREE."

"Whew. It's just full of old clothes." Melody sighed as they opened the lid.

"Of course it is," Eddie said. "See? This is Uncle Jasper's old hat."

"That's the hat we saw in the window," Howie said slowly.

"Have you flipped?" Eddie said as he tried to put on the hat. "Hey! This won't fit."

"It's probably because your head is so big." Melody giggled.

"No, really. Look. Something's stuck under the lining," Eddie told them. He took off the hat and tugged at the material. It was so old it tore with very little pulling.

All the kids gulped when they saw what was inside the hat.

11

Hats Off to Uncle Jasper

"Wow!" Melody shrieked.

"There must be a million bucks in here," Eddie whistled as he thumbed through the wad of hundred dollar bills. "We're rich!"

"That's not OUR money," Melody told him. "It's Aunt Mathilda's."

"She doesn't even know it's here," Eddie snapped. "Uncle Jasper must have hidden it."

"It's still hers," Howie said firmly. "And she needs the money!"

"If you think I'm going to turn over all this dough to Aunt Mathilda, you've got bats in your belfry," Eddie told her.

Melody shook her finger at Eddie. "You're just as greedy as your Uncle Jasper."

"How can you even think of taking money from her? She may be in the hospital for weeks!" Liza said.

"Aw, I guess you're right," Eddie sighed. "But maybe she'll give us a reward."

"Eddie, you're hopeless." Melody started piling the money into an empty shoe box.

"We're lucky the light was on in the attic," Howie said. "Or we wouldn't have found the hat."

"It's almost as if someone wanted us to find it," Melody said slowly.

Liza nodded. "Jasper's ghost did. He had to help us find the money he hid from Aunt Mathilda so he could rest. If he were here we could thank him."

Eddie snickered. "Miss Manners herself, Emily P. Ghost!"

"Liza's right," Howie said slowly. "Maybe we should thank him."

Liza shook her head. "I don't think we'll find Uncle Jasper's ghost."

"Why not?" Howie asked.

Liza shrugged. "His wrong has been righted. He can rest now."

12

Coincidence?

Two months later, the four kids stared at Aunt Mathilda's house. "It looks great," Melody said.

"It is wonderful," Liza agreed. The old house didn't look the same. The roof was fixed and the windows were sparkling. New green paint covered the house and the shutters were a bright clean white.

The cheerful red door swung open and Aunt Mathilda waved at the four kids. She looked much better since coming home from the hospital. She wore jeans and a T-shirt, and her gray hair was tucked under a Bailey Elementary baseball cap.

"Don't just stand there," she bellowed. "Come in and let's play poker!"

Everyone laughed as they opened the new gate and walked up the steps.

"If it hadn't been for Jasper's hat, this house would've collapsed with the first snowflake," Melody laughed.

"It was lucky we found it," Howie said.

"That wasn't luck," Liza said quietly. "Jasper's ghost helped us find it."

"Naw, it was just dumb luck," Eddie said.

"I guess you're right," Melody admitted. "It was silly to think he could've been a ghost."

Howie laughed. "After all, ghosts don't eat potato chips!"